Walter Sweetman

The Daughters of the King, and Other Poems

Being a sequel to Through the night and Onward

Walter Sweetman

The Daughters of the King, and Other Poems
Being a sequel to Through the night and Onward

ISBN/EAN: 9783337212780

Printed in Europe, USA, Canada, Australia, Japan

Cover: Foto ©Andreas Hilbeck / pixelio.de

More available books at **www.hansebooks.com**

THE

DAUGHTERS OF THE KING

AND OTHER POEMS

BEING A SEQUEL TO 'THROUGH THE NIGHT' AND 'ONWARD'

BY

WALTER SWEETMAN, B.A.

LONDON

LONGMANS, GREEN, AND CO.

1871

PREFACE.

I BEGAN THE PREFACE to my first literary effort[1] with the name of Félicité Robert de Lamennais, and with thought of him I commence a few remarks introductory to the following pages. Can it be that the Papal Allocution which was the occasion of his ruin was not an infallible pronouncement after all? Might he have listened in respectful silence, as became a dutiful son of the Church, and kept his thoughts and worked out his problems as Galileo did before him, and with the same result? I know this is a very terrible thing to write. I am sure many well-intentioned people might be made really angry by reading it. Fortunately I am not myself much afraid of indignation when severed from right; and having a strong hope and opinion

[1] *Through the Night* and *Onward:* Longmans, 1869.

that the ' oratorical ' phrases of the ' Mirari Vos '
were not the inspired voice of the Roman Catholic
Church, I will try to set down here the reasons
which induce me to entertain both the one and the
other. We liberal Catholics have been having a
hard time enough of it with all sides. Protestants
have been claiming our best men again and again,
while high authorities in our own Church have
publicly ranked us with lukewarm Catholics and
with *bad* Catholics. Our best answer is probably to
state facts, and to reason on them. I have an im-
pression that we are the winners after all.

To begin with, if people are so wedded to their
own views as to be even *astonished* when others
assign their plain natural meaning to words pro-
nounced by the very highest authority, with them
it is almost useless to argue. To give an instance.
We read in page 188 of the January number of the
' Dublin Review,' the following passage referring to
the late decision of a general council :—

' We find, however, with extreme surprise, that an
important passage in the preamble has been understood to signify that papal infallibility is limited to
an exposition of those verities which are actually

contained in Scripture and tradition. It is of the utmost moment to rectify this misapprehension; and we begin, therefore, with quoting at length the passage to which reference is made:—

' " *The Roman Pontiffs (have from time to time) defined as to be held those things which with the help of God they had recognised as conformable with the sacred Scriptures and Apostolic tradition. For the Holy Spirit was not promised to the successors of Peter that by his revelation they might disclose new doctrine, but that by his assistance they might inviolably keep and faithfully expound the Revelation or Deposit of Faith delivered to the Apostles.*" '

Why should the writer be extremely *surprised* that here black should be held to mean black and white white? He does not even pretend that the natural meaning of the words would contradict some other passage of this most solemn of all documents. He merely says that it will be seen at once that such an ' interpretation ' would prove too much, because ' If by the phrase new doctrines papally undefinable were designated all doctrinal statements without exception which are not contained in Scripture and

tradition, what would follow on such an hypothesis?
It would be "a new doctrine" papally undefinable
that Jansenius's book contains five certain propositions in its legitimate objective sense; it would be
a new doctrine papally undefinable that this or that
canonized person is a saint; it would be a new doctrine papally undefinable that the Council of Trent
is Œcumenical.'

Now does this prove too much? Why should a
supernatural infallibility be required to decide
whether a certain book contained a certain doctrine
or not? The point upon which supernatural illumi-
nation was required was whether the doctrine was
sound or unsound. As to the rest, it was a mere
matter of fact; and if the proper authorities in the
Church are sure that the book did contain this per-
nicious matter, have they not the power of excom-
municating all who read it, which will answer every
purpose. Again, in the very improbable case that a
saint, so to speak, is not a saint, what great harm is
done? God sees the faith of the humble believer,
and gives to it the reward it deserves. How can we
draw a distinction between the devotion to a saint
who is not a saint, and devotion to a miracle which

is not a miracle? The only distinction is, that the first is a much more *un*likely contingency than the last. Was anybody the worse for honouring the water of La Salette, although one of the two witnesses of the so-called wonder confessed to the Curé of Ars that he was an impostor? In the same way, when the Church knows that one of her general councils was Œcumenical, surely she can excommunicate those who would deny it. Where, in any one of these three cases, is there the necessity for a supernatural pronouncement so imperative as to require that the most solemn words of the Church should be understood in a sense directly contrary to their natural meaning? The writer's other argument, that the individual bishops who composed the majority of the council were of his opinion, is no argument at all. As Catholics, we are bound to believe that it was not they, but the Holy Ghost, who spoke. At all events it is hard to see any reasonable ground for extreme *surprise* in the matter.

And now to come to the words of the definition itself. Nothing could seem to be simpler or plainer. They are:

'We teach and define that it is a divinely revealed

dogma that the Roman Pontiff, when he speaks *ex
cathedrâ*—that is, when in discharge of his office of
pastor and doctor of all Christians he defines in
virtue of his supreme apostolic authority, a doctrine
of faith or morals to be held by the Universal
Church—is endowed by the Divine assistance promised to him in blessed Peter *with that infallibility
with which our Divine Redeemer willed that the
Church should be furnished in defining doctrine of
faith or morals.*'

The italics are my own ; but the fact is plain, if
words can be plain, that the infallibility which the
Pope possesses is that with which the Church
is furnished for *defining* doctrine of faith and
morals ; and what is to define a doctrine of faith
and morals but to terminate with scientific and
judicial accuracy some question regarding them, as
Honorius certainly did not terminate the controversy
about the wills of our Lord, and, as I would suggest,
Gregory XVI. did not in the ' Mirari Vos ' point out
the bounds of the rights of conscience or of the
necessary relationship of Church and State.

This, then, is my proposition—-that the Council
of the Vatican has decided that the Pope speaks *ex*

cathedrâ only when he defines or sets out with scientific and judicial accuracy some certain doctrine of faith and morals to be held by the whole Church, having stated in the preamble that as a matter of fact he only does this in the case of doctrines revealed to the Apostles. I believe this to be true on the simple ground that it is the plain meaning of the words. I also hope it to be true, for many reasons, which I shall now proceed to explain.

In the first place, the simple rendering of the words will remove all fair excuse for the habit which many good conscientious people have of regarding what they profess to be the voice of the Holy Ghost as a strange and unaccountable fact, which is not to have the slightest effect upon their real convictions. There is, I should think, scarcely an educated Catholic layman in this country but would laugh to scorn the suggestion that under any circumstances he could be obliged in conscience to restrict the religious liberties of his Protestant neighbours, while he will tell you with the same breath that he believes (of course he does) in the ' Mirari Vos,' and that you are a great fool to trouble your head about it. Now either the Holy Ghost speaks in that Bull about our political duties or He does not. If He does not, it was not an infallible pronouncement; if He does, I am not a fool to trouble my head about it.

In the second place, I hope that the plain words can be taken in their plain meaning, because such a construction will remove all the difficulties which arise from what our adversaries call our infallible blunders. It is now an article of faith that the Pope never did blunder *ex cathedrâ*. But it is a notorious fact that he has blundered in grave pronouncements and on the most important matters, and I should like to know what distinction can be drawn that will so satisfactorily explain these facts as the distinctions that are presented to us by assigning their plain and natural meaning to these inspired words. The Pope speaks infallibly when he sets forth a doctrine of faith or morals with scientific and judicial accuracy as Honorius set forth none, and this only in so far as that doctrine is purely of faith and supernatural morals, and therefore he could blunder in questions of astronomy or of political economy, but not blunder *ex cathedrâ*, having, by the very fact of entering on them, gone out of his proper position. I believe these two principles will meet every difficulty which can be raised by our adversaries, and they are both in the fullest degree consonant with natural reason. One of the very first things we should expect to find in a great lawgiver is distinctness of precept, and why should the greatest of all be an exception ? Again, why should a supernatural authority be required for matters which fairly fall within the cognisance of our natural powers ? If the Church had but decided that it was criminal to avail oneself of the temporary want of one's neighbour to extort an unfair profit out of him, she would be fairly within her powers ; but when she decided that some certain interest or any interest at all *was* an unfair extortion, she passed into the territories of natural science, and by that very fact ceased to be infallible.

I have dwelt upon this matter at some length because I have a strong belief that the very greatest evil of our times is to be found in the wrong views of good Catholics upon the means by which they should propagate their faith. They have but too often forgotten, as it seems to me, that the true foundations of religious strength are moral and intellectual, and that if the mere physical superstructure is

extended at the expense of those foundations, the whole edifice is just so much the nearer to a fall. Does it never strike a good Ultramontane—I am using the word in its modern sense—that by committing the infallibility of the Church to a great natural wrong, such, for instance, as the duty of infringing on the rights of conscience, he has weakened her cause? Can there be a greater impiety than to try to make the God of Revelation speak against the God of Nature?

I have myself no doubt whatever but that they have just been mining the ground under their own feet. By the very means they have taken to increase their physical strength, they have thrown it away. Whatever else Ultramontanism may have effected, it has succeeded, and is succeeding, in weakening the Latin nations. Without speaking here of some other of their views, which necessarily set the two strongest of these nations one against the other, is it too much to say that the man who in these times defends religious persecution is a bad citizen? If they would but become liberal, if they would but cease to try to help the Church against God and His justice, I am convinced that they might convert the world. The rational beauty of Catholic Christianity, when seen undeformed by the devices of men, must attract every mind and every heart. For God's sake let us cease to make our religion unamiable and absurd by unnecessary difficulties and repulsive theories which have long outlived the facts which they were invented to produce. Our faith is, even naturally speaking, the most magnificent conception of the human mind. I am not preaching what I do not practise; I have done my very best—and, as children say, who can do more?— to transmit some faint shade of that beauty to the following pages. They are intended to form a part— and if really poetry, they do form a part—of the demonstration of those two propositions which in the preface to my first volumes I said I believed that I was able to prove.

In conclusion, I wish to state that there is one sentence which I regret to have written. It contains an allusion to Ananias and Sapphira, is to be found in page 102 of my second volume, and is lamentably weak.

I may also, perhaps, be allowed to say that I have changed my mind to some extent on the subject o.

university education; and believe that the best system for Ireland is that which will unite religious teaching with unsectarian examination, as at London, due allowance being made in the apportioning both of funds and examiners to the numbers educated successfully by the different religions, and care being taken to give all a fair start.

Of this I may speak more at large if I ever resume the story of ' Onward,' whose development it would be more charitable to suppose I have awaited rather than forgotten. Speaking of charity, which should begin by justice, I do not think it is fair to take my thoughts without acknowledgment.

A very able writer in the last number of the ' Edinburgh Review' winds up an article on Mr. Darwin, by suggesting that while his system may have thrown some new light on the evolution of man's body, it altogether fails to account for the existence of his soul. This means simply that Adam's body may have been formed, or may appear to have been formed, through a long line of apes, in preparation for that gift of soul which made the man, and is a view which I endeavoured to put forward in the tenth chapter of my second volume.

I remonstrated with this gentleman through our common publishers, but was only referred magnificently to a page of St. Augustine. I have examined it, but found, of course, that that great man had not the remotest idea of Adam's father having been a highly developed brute. On the contrary, he expressly writes, ' ut illud tantum proprium habuerat quod non ex parentibus natus est, sed factus ex terra,' and compares the formation of his body to the change of water into wine at Cana. Now I believe the idea or view referred to is destined to be of great importance; and though it is quite possible that some one may have struck on it before me, as far as I know I am the first to give it plainly to the world. As far I am myself concerned it is completely original, and under these circumstances I claim for it the protection of honourable men.

WALTER SWEETMAN

CONTENTS.

THE DAUGHTERS OF THE KING.

'And all the days of Mathusala were nine hundred
and sixty nine years : and he died.'

GENESIS, chap. v. verse 27.

PERSONS.

SALEPH . . . *A Patriarch.*

SETH ⎫
AMOS ⎭ . . . . *Sons to Saleph.*

ARVAH ⎫
HEVIRAH ⎭ . *Maidens of the tribe of Cain.*

Act I.

SCENE I.

A grassy mountain slope.   Above, a forest and rocks.
On one side a deep fissure.

Amos and Seth.

AMOS.

Here let us sit a while
And watch the plain drink in the evening sun,
Smiling as we smile when we drink at night
The red juice of our vines.

SETH.

So be it then.
This hour my legs have aped our father's age.
Why must we thus grow old ?

AMOS.

Because of sin
And death.

SETH.

But we sinned not—nor you nor I.

AMOS.

Not yet, it may be.   In our simple lives,
Tending our flock or wooing our young fields,
Far from the converse of our fallen kind,
And with our father's voice like that of God,
'Tis hard to sin.

SETH.

And yet our brother died
Writhing with torture.

AMOS.

One of the mysteries.
Perhaps each pang was germ of joy eternal ;
Perhaps we all have sown the seeds of crime
That should bear fruit had not God taken him.

SETH.

First punishing for that he did not do.
I cannot fathom it.

AMOS.

Who can ?   Oh, Seth,
Look out on the great world, and think of Him
Who drew it forth from nothing. Who may fathom
His ways?   He made us: then 'tis ours to listen—
To listen and believe.

SETH.

You have said well.

If I have spoken aught that doth offend,
I am sorry.   Adam sinned, and that was much.
E'en now men that God made but live to sin.
Lo where it spreads out in His own bright sun—
From this green slope we see it plainer still—
Yon sea of roofs—the cursed roofs of Cain.
I've that to tell you on this eve—nay, now—
That well might make their sheen seem glimmer of
    hell.
For twice a hundred years no male born child
Hath lived within those walls: they sacrifice
Them all to Moloch.

AMOS.

What!   Not their own sons?

SETH.

Yes, their own sons.   They have no natural love,
Those fierce old men, the cruel breed of Cain.
A brother's blood branded their father's brow,
And now in deadliest descent of ill
They slay their future rivals in their sons.
Hereto our father's will forbade me frame
In words such act; but now that he hath joined you
In this my journey, he hath bade me speak,

And I have spoken, knowing well you wiser
In many things than I, though I am elder,
And stronger as I think; but let that pass.
There is a poison in those walls that needs
An antidote in knowledge—such his words—
Poison in all the air.   From morn till night
Young girls are twining through their streets in dance
Before some idol that they bear along.
I walk with downcast eyes, I scarce know why,
When I have thus to tread the hated ground,
Feeling to gaze were treason to the Lord.

AMOS.

Ay, to the Lord of Nature, that made man,
Female and male, that each finding in each
Its mystic complement might pair in friendship
Fruitful and pure and endless as in heaven.

SETH.

And yet I would we all were men: then had been
Perhaps no sin.

AMOS.

Peace, Seth!   We had a mother.
Poor mother! that hath died and left no trace
Save in one memory.

SETH.

My father's, Amos?

AMOS.

Ay, Seth, our father.   Long ago I heard—
My bed being nearest and my sleep less sound—
Him sighing when I woke, and knew ere long
Wherefore he grieved and prayed.   Now he grows
　　feebler,
He wakes the more, and prays, but sighs the less.

SETH.

She was a daughter of the Sons of God,
Pure and unspotted, with no fetid drop
Of Cain's black blood.   But for those wicked ones—
Oft think I, Amos, would the Lord would send
Us down with club and sword to smite them all,
You with your staff, and me with my good sword,
Till none were left to do Him injury.

AMOS.

What! but we two against the multitude?

SETH.

Ay, we two and the Lord.   I tell you, brother,
If He commanded that we raze yon cliffs,
They'd melt before us like the morning mist.
One man with Him may strive against a thousand.
For one day, as I slept in yonder walls
In the fierce noontide heat, a sudden tumult

Awoke me, and I sprang up, as a girl
Crouched to my side, an infant in her arms—
An infant that the fiends sought for their gods.
I drew my sword and smote, and as they came
On rushing, smote and smote, and had no wound.
I felt the great Archangel held his shield
Above me as I strove.　And lo the woman
Pushed through a loophole in the outer wall
And dropped down with her man-child in her arms.
And then they left me, and I had no wound,
But walked about the streets and did my will,
And no man injured me ; but as I passed
From out the city gate with my piled mule,
A little child, a little graceful child,
Ran out and threw a chain upon my neck
And then was gone—a heavy chain of gold.
I gave it to my father, and he counselled silence,
But changed that bidding too last night.

AMOS.

　　　　　　　　　　It may be
He feared I seeing you thus chosen of Heaven
Might grieve less favoured.

SETH.

　　　　　　　　And now, wiser grown,
Fears it no more.

AMOS.

He need have never feared.
Since first we climbed the trees about our hut
I've had a joy in your bold deeds.   Oft then
I'd lie upon the grass to gaze half giddy
Upon your laughing daring as you rose.

SETH.

I have no fear of death—rather of sickness,
Age, and decrepitude.   Had I my will,
It were to die unbent ere yet——
                              [*A peal of thunder is heard.*
                    Thunder!
And the clear sun is all undimmed.

AMOS.

                    The clouds
Are working up behind.   'Tis time we looked
After our mules.

SETH.

                    One moment, ere we go.
There is a thought that sometimes puzzles me:
How is it, brother, that the Lord, being good
And justice infinite, can love the pain
And blood of things that do no ill?   If we
Who sinned must die, why should they die who
    sinned not,

And die a bloody death in sacrifice?
I often grudge my poor lambs to the knife.

AMOS.

I think our father sees.

SETH.

Why hide it then?

AMOS.

I know not.   It may be he dares not open
Such depth of thoughts divine to you and me.
When I've so questioned him a glow of love
Made his brow beautiful beyond its wont,
And, laying his thin hand upon my head,
He said, 'My son, thou too mayest know some day;'
But other answer made he none.

SETH.

'Tis strange.

AMOS.

Most things are strange.   And yet you said but now
You would like well to be God's holocaust;
For so I deem your words might stand interpreted.

SETH.

Ay, but in battle freely, not like a slave.

AMOS.

Then you, being good and brave, deserve the pain
Less than your lambs.

SETH.

I cannot reason on it.
I only know I feel that He is good
Beyond all thought and compassing of man,
And I His soldier.

[*A cry of hounds beneath.*

AMOS.

Hark below!

SETH.

Their dogs.
They train them to pursue the fleeing deer,
And men and women follow in their wake
Shouting encouragement.

AMOS.

Not the soft deer—
The gentle mild-eyed deer?   Have they no wolves,
Tigers, or lions, if they must take life?

SETH.

And yet it is a race, limb against limb,
That well may fire the blood.   See where it comes—
The quarry toiling upwards through yon rocks.

AMOS.

And now the barking of the dogs draws nearer—
Not a loud bark, as though they felt their strength
Needed for deeds, not sounds. There, there they
   come!—
There, by yon outer pine-trees—three, four, five,
In single line winding amid the stones,
Still keeping to the track with keener sense
Than God has given to man.   So oft perchance
The evil ones pursue a hard-set soul
With gaping fang, and almost mute at last
In their dread hate and keen expectancy.
Lo now!

SETH.

     The deer! the hunted deer!   Poor wretch!
How it has crouched against the rocks beneath us,
As though it asked for pity.

AMOS.

       And I do pity.
Why should men torture thus a blameless beast,
That but this morn was happy?   Now, by Heaven,
I may not choose but help it.

SETH.

Stay! stay! —— He's gone,
And soon will have the hunters swarming round

Like hornets.   Come, old sword : we'll stand by him
If worst comes worst.

SCENE II.

The rocks below.

ARVAH, SETH, and AMOS.

ARVAH.

What! both at one?   Then I, too, wait for odds.

SETH.

You lie, girl, if a girl you are.   I stayed
Your blows—that only.

ARVAH.

    Then stand you aside,
And let him strike.

SETH.

   He wars not with a girl.

ARVAH.

Girl! When yon stag first sprang out from his lair,
A hundred hounds leaped down upon the track,
And all the woods resounded with the shouts
Of hurrying men.   Where are they now?   A girl!
What good is there in man that I have not?
Strength, courage, swiftness, I have all.   The rest

Is but the cruelty and wrong that's born
Of strength.   These have I not, nor wish to have.

AMOS.

Then why war thus upon that gentle beast?

ARVAH.

Why slay the gentler ones your shepherds tend?
I warred upon no beast.   It was my dogs,
That did their nature's bidding.   Rail at her—
Nature—not me.   I did but follow them
To make my young step firm, my breathing sure,
E'en as you eat your sheep to make you strong.

AMOS.

My nature bade me save the deer.

ARVAH.

And kill
The dog that was my friend; that lay by me
At night, and would have died to save my finger;
That lived but for my love and praise.   I tell you,
When all at fault the baffled pack was dumb,
And he would strike the track as was his wont,
Those poor dead eyes would turn to me in triumph.
You shall have vengeance, friend! Stranger, if man
You are, why, show yourself a man.   Your blood
Or mine!

AMOS.

Mine be it then.   I will not strive
With you ; but I can die.   If blood must flow,
Take mine.

SETH.

Brother, you are mad ; you know them not—
The cruel race.   [*To Arvah.*]   By Heaven ! you
may not strike.

ARVAH.

'Tis true, I may not.   Fool, drop you that sword !
His is the deeper insight.   Fare you well,
Poor dog, poor faithful wretch !   I go, old friend.
And now, you boaster, see what girl can do.
                    [*She leaps across the fissure.*
Farewell.   A storm is brewing.   There is shelter
This side, but you would fear the leap.

SETH.

By Heaven ! she braves us with that scoff.   I'll follow
her.

AMOS.

You must not.   'Tis a desperate leap.

SETH.

                              More shameful
If I follow not.

SCENE III.

A cavern in the mountain. Storm outside. Thunder and lightning.

Enter SETH.

SETH.

How the light flickers down the uneven roof,
Glancing and shivering till it fade far off
In stars on fretted sea ! Great Heaven, the thunder !
That peal might split the solid mountain down.
Perchance 'twas such another split it once,
And made the chasm I leaped. I earned my shelter:
So I'll tell Amos when we meet. 'Twas stout of him
To save the deer. I did not think his prudence
Could be so rash. If all the hunters came,
We had a merry time of it ere now.
That I will tell him too. Again a flash !
And almost at its heels the terrible roar.
'Twas not for nothing that the night came thus.
I often wonder why my father sent me,
Not him, upon this errand—ever me.
Yet he has such a long head, always thinking
And puzzling over this and that, until
Our father's self I ween is scarce as wise.

I know 'tis pleasant that he comes at last.
It was a dismal thing to be alone
In the accursed place.   I always found
Each hour a day ere yet the —— What a blaze!
There are no loose stones upward, else the crash
Might well have sent them tumbling on my head.
It lit up vasty distances beyond,
All rough and rugged as where now I stand.
And here another cave burrows this way.
A feeble glimmer! yes, by Heaven, a light!
And as I turn a shrouded form crouching
Beside a lamp—a weird form, motionless
As are the dead under the funeral sheet,
And with the face so veiled.   From far-off darkness
Comes a faint murmuring of hollow sound.
A most strange tomb, if—— Surely then it moved;
Speak! what art thou?

WOMAN.
That which was once a girl.

SETH.
A woman!

WOMAN.
What is left of one.   And you?

SETH.
A man.

* C

WOMAN.

A man?   Nay, let me gaze at you.
A man, with that smooth cheek and youthful brow?
A man?

SETH.

Why what of these?

WOMAN.

I think you mock.
You are of those strange things that play at men,
Aping the daughter of a king.

SETH.

Look at me.
When I have walked the streets of Cain, I've met
Few there as large as I.

WOMAN.

I hear and know
You for a man indeed.

SETH.

What, by my voice?

WOMAN.

No: by your words.

SETH.

Yours have a jibing ring.

WOMAN.

I jibe.

SETH.

Who and what are you?

WOMAN.

Priestess here,

That for a hundred years have seen no face
Like yours.

SETH.

Priestess?   What demon do you serve?

WOMAN.

Myself and my own misery, that loves
To gnaw men's crimes as jackals gnaw old bones.

SETH.

While Moloch has the lion's share!

WOMAN.

I doubt it.

I doubt there be a Moloch.   'Tis the name
We give to our own wickedness.

SETH.

Who has?

WOMAN.

The destiny that's born of crime—the something
That without crime is not.

SETH.

Have you none such?

WOMAN.

Ha! Ha!

SETH.

Why do you laugh?

WOMAN.

Just my good humour—
For fifty years I'm priestess here.   For four
Times fifty every male born child dies here.
Here, too, the mothers die that would evade
Our law. Would you know how? I ll take my lamp
And show.

SETH.

Strange lamp!   Around a bitten apple
A serpent twines and twines, its hissing mouth
The channel of the wick.

WOMAN.

Is it so strange?
I'll show you stranger things.   Look down!

SETH.

I look.

It is a fissure I have leaped outside,
That thus crosses the cave. I just can make out
The clammy walls, black and precipitate.

WOMAN.

Not so.   The mountain here is rent throughout
With such.   Look down.

SETH.

I do.

WOMAN.

What see you now?

SETH.

Nothing except the slippery rocks, but hear,
Deep in the bowels of the earth, a roar
Of water, that would seem to splash and fall,
I ween from mountain cliff (and I have tried)
Few may look down so far.

WOMAN.

It is a vein

Of the great earth, that there surges and frets.
Water is nature's blood.

SETH.

Whence can it come?
And whence the sickening odour that pervades
The place, so loathsome, deathly, horrible?

WOMAN.

Tush!   One thing at a time.   As for the water,
It springs from the deep-caverned womb of earth—

Perchance may be a river that has dipped
Into the earth.   It breaks out miles below,
A poisoned stream.   Old legends say it came first
With man from heaven.   If so, it, like the other,
Is worse for wear.

SETH.

I do remember now
I saw its gleam afar, when late I sat
Upon the mountain-side.   How strange!

WOMAN.

There are
Much stranger things.   The topmost dome of all
Beyond the city is a hollow cone,
A mighty funnel, whose unsounded depths
Boil with a fount of living fire.   Perchance
The earth's a giant that once did great wrong,
And now must burn at heart for ever, while we,
Its parasites, live out our little lives
Upon the suffering frame.

SETH.

It could not live.

WOMAN.

And why?

SETH.

It has nor mouth nor ears nor eyes.

WOMAN.

Ha! ha!

SETH.

You laugh.

WOMAN.

My way of showing wonder.

SETH.

At what?

WOMAN.

At wisdom.   Have you never seen
A crystal that reflects—that will give back
Your face, for instance, if you hold it near?

SETH.

No.

WOMAN.

Then I have ; but, look you, hold it near
A mountain and it gives not that.

SETH.

Your meaning?

WOMAN.

Our fancies, with their ears and nose and eyes,
Are but the crystal, the great earth the mountain.

SETH.

You laugh at me.   I leaped a chasm outside
As wide as this.

WOMAN.

Ha! ha! I've seen a flea
Do quite as much and more in its proportion.
But listen.   Hearest thou aught of change?

SETH.

Nothing.

WOMAN.

Men have thus listened for three hundred years,
And heard no change. Down this we throw our
    children.

SETH.

Demon!

WOMAN.

For the weak mothers that would save them
We have a sterner ending.   Hold the lamp
Now to its highest, that the light may fall
Beyond.   What see you there?

SETH.

A rugged nook
Worn in the solid rock, as though the cavern
Just reached across and ended.   I can trace
Its outlines.

WOMAN.

Look again.

SETH.

I think I see
Some dark thing stretched along the further side.

WOMAN.

It is the wretch last punished. She was just
Alive an hour ago. A weakly thing
That dared not fling herself from her great pain
Down as most do. She must be almost dead
Of hunger now. We stretch this plank across,
Then leave them in the rock. They often tear
Their fingers to the bone scratching against it.

SETH.

Demon, beware ! It may be that my man's blood
Can bear no more, but hurl you to your victims.

WOMAN.

Ha ! ha ! Then will there be one woman less—
A very old one.

SETH.

Fearest thou nothing ?

WOMAN.

Say rather
I fear all things so much I have no choice
Of ills. But, look you, if you slay me here,
They'll find another crone that once was young,

Half crazed with thinking of the joys she knew
And others know, but she can know no more.
And she will be their priestess just as I,
And joy in pain as I, your trouble lost.
Rather, since yours such manly rage and strength—
There is the plank you see—stretch it across
And rescue that poor weakling while you may.
So—deftly done—now venture boldly on.
Hold! are you tired of life, rash, witless man?

[*She drops her disguise and appears as Arvah.*]

Were she I mimicked here, you were as trapped
As yon poor corse.   See, thus I push the plank
Down the abyss; hear how it rattles.   Well
For thee thou standest on this side, not that.

SETH.

So it is you!

ARVAH.

                    Was that the splash?   Fool! fool!
Were the old priestess here whose shroud and lamp
I found and borrowed, yours were sterner fate
Than even I could wish.   Keep to your hills,
Or mend your ways, you and your brother; else,
By Cain, your days will be but few.

SETH (*pointing to the body*).

                                        And can we
For her do nothing human?

ARVAH.

Who is dead, is dead.

SETH.

She is dead, then?

ARVAH.

The thing must be a skeleton.
When it was clothed with flesh, it edified
Us all by its decease, some six months back.

SETH.

Come to the air; it is too horrible!

ARVAH.

For you perhaps; for me it has its lessons.

SETH.

Lessons! But I must get back to my brother.
For God's sake, let us leave this devilish place.

ARVAH.

God's sake! What God?

SETH.

What God! Still I forget—
'Tis time I sought my brother. Though the storm
Is passed, the light scarce marks the cavern's mouth.

ARVAH.

And therefore without guide you may not find
Your path among the cliffs.   Bide where you are
Until the morning dawn.   I seek the city.
Till then the cave is yours.

SETH.
                          The moon will soon

Have risen.

ARVAH.
                     The chasm you leaped bars your return;
The pass is hard to find.   Come, as I owe you
Somewhat for this great fright, I'll show the way.

SETH.

On, then.   I long to be with something good.
I do not mean to be discourteous, maiden,
But your ways are not ours.

ARVAH.
                          Yet have yours blood.

You wear a sword.

SETH.
                     Ay, and have used it too

In honest battle, striving for the right.

ARVAH.

And yet now fear to be alone with me,
Lest, turning to some dismal shape, I grin
And frighten yon to death.

SETH.

              I do not fear,
But long to see my brother's face again,
And hear his voice.

ARVAH.

           Why, what weak thing you are,
With all your boasting!   Were he here, I ween,
He would not long for your big company!
When my sword crossed his staff I felt his strength—
The strength of heart that would not strive with
   me—
While you—ay, in your inmost soul—you longed
To meet me as a man should meet a man,
Despite your mighty words.

SETH.

           Let us go on!
Yourself doth teach me how a man should bear
With these words now.

ARVAH.

          An apt disciple, truly!
And thus we gain the cavern's mouth at last.
See how the moon peeps o'er yon glistening rock
To light our forward steps, while the great earth
Drips like a giant from a bath! Poor hot,
Hot-hearted giant! Let us go! But tell me,
Why wear you not a chain of gold? 'Tis mean
To be so plain.

SETH.

    I have a chain at home.

ARVAH.

Then why not wear it?

SETH.

        Thus my father wishes.

ARVAH.

And you, great man, do all your father wishes?

SETH.

Surely I do.

ARVAH.

    You have said well: your ways
Are not as our ways. Let us go. I—I too
Have one that waiteth for me, pure and good

As is your vaunted brother—one who now
Perchance is looking from our roof in wonder
That Arvah cometh not, she and her dog,
Poor dog that ne'er will come again!

SCENE IV.

Another part of the mountain. Two mules picketed among rocks; in front of them AMOS.

AMOS.

He is so swiftfooted,
And sure to follow her, if but to show
He risked the leap. I cannot doubt they met.
Could she have lured him to an ambush? She!
She lured him not. Scarce might I ward her blows,
So the strange beauty of her dark young face
Possessed me as I stood. She lured him not.
More like they sheltered from the storm together.
How gracefully she struck and ran and leaped!
Agile as Seth, but with a subtle form
So different—a woman's form. A woman!
Woman! that great half of our kind, my sire
Hath fled from with his sons, for so I read
His life. From woman most he fled. A girl!
The word that ever makes my secret soul

Vibrate with a strange longing, half of fear!
A girl! How sorrowful she was through all
Her rage and scorn! Would that my hand were seared
Ere it had smote the dog! What was the deer
To me, that I should do her so much wrong?
And yet when I caught then its gentle gaze
Fixed on my face so thankfully, I could
Not choose but feel a joy that it was safe.
Most cruel earth, where all things are at war,
And we can scarcely help without destroying!
'Blame Nature and not me.' And what is Nature?
I almost had said, Who? Oh, Seth, my brother,
Whose doubts and questions are but flitting ever
As breeze and ripple o'er the constant depth
Of your great love, did you but guess how oft
The answer that I give so readily
Is but from one side of my vexèd mind,
That strives with all my will for mastery,
You'd know me better than you do. My father
Reads deeper: hence his greater love for Seth.
With Seth he finds the trust and peace unshaken
In which his travel-wearied soul may freshen.
Poor father! who hath suffered much, most then
When she he loved was taken in her youth,
'Tis hard indeed to bear such blow and feel
The hand that strikes is Goodness infinite,
Then most good when it strikes. I often think now

God lets her spirit breathe itself through his
By sweet persuasion and suggested word ;
For it can scarce be natural to man
To be as kind and fond as he.   Perhaps
Who love, unbodied seek the souls they love,
Mingling more deeply than before.   Who may tell
Whence come our thoughts, which are our own,
   which spirits',
Evil or good, that thus hold converse with us ?
So she with him.   I would not know my mother.
I wonder was her face like that to-night.
Methinks I see it more in my dear father's
When he is sad—softer and sad.
                                      The light
Hath faded westward, and our one-week's moon,
Peeping beneath the lifting thunder-cloud,
Makes an enchanted pathway to the east.
Such lustrous track the angels may have left
In the old times, from Eden to their stars
Returning—times when man was as an angel,
And he too knew——
                          Surely I heard a voice,
The distant murmur of a voice, below
Among the rocks.   The mules have heard it too,
And listen with pricked ears.   Again !—'tis she,
And Seth is following.   How his shoulders stretch
Broadly beyond her as he comes !   All's well.

'Twas good of her to point the way; for so
I read her presence.   They are silent now.

Enter SETH and ARVAH.

SETH.

Oh, Amos, I have seen such things!

AMOS.

But are

Unhurt ?

SETH.

Things horrible beyond all thought,
Blacker than worst imagining of man.
Methinks till now I scarce felt half their horror,
Thus seeing you.

I've looked upon the spot
Where women that would save their sons are starved
By inches in a stone cell o'er a chasm
Deeper and darker than the one we leaped.
Were there one human heart in all the tribe,
It were not done.

ARVAH.

Thou liest!

SETH.

The plank I stretched across—
A child could do as much.

ARVAH.

              Then were it child
That had good mind to take the other's place.

SETH.

There was no guard.

ARVAH.

            Upon that body, true.
You might have stretched ten planks across, and she
Would not have stirred.

AMOS.

            Surely you must see, brother,
Men are the stronger : what they will, they do.

SETH.

Better to die than suffer wrongs like those.

ARVAH.

Better to win than die.

SETH.

            And be a slave
Meanwhile.

ARVAH.

        Not so.   But mark, I've left you safe
Here with your brother. I must go. Farewell.

AMOS.

First share our homely meal—hard cakes and honey,
And wine that cools in yonder rushing stream.

ARVAH.

I thank you; but I go. I'm waited for.
I wandered far out of my path to help
My fellow-leaper here. [*To* SETH.] Here is my hand—
An honest hand. Take it—no slaves. Good night.
If I can serve you in your quest to-morrow,
I will.

SETH.

        We need no help : our wool we barter,
Taking back hand-wrought goods.

ARVAH.

                        Then once again
Good night. Next time I see you, you must wear
Your chain of gold.

SETH.

        Next time ?   And when shall that be ?

Act II.

SCENE I.

A grove on the plains.

SALEPH.

    'The first that mounts the hill :'
So said the voice—surely I heard it then—
The voice that I have ever held of God.
Another taken from me in his prime!
Another! Which? Ah me! another face
Gone from our life!
       And yet for this I live,
For this have striven through all the weary years.
Since first their opening reasons clung to mine
I've sought to twine the tendrils round His love,
Man's solitary stay.   When the bright morns
Of springtime called us to the fields, I've waked
Them ever with a prayer to Him who gives

The grain its increase and the young their strength ;
And when the autumn sun looked down at last
Upon the golden glory of the corn,
Bronzing their open bosoms as they toiled,
And glittering on the sheaves, I prayed again
That they might be His wheat, and glitter too
In glory of full ripeness evermore.
And now, my prayer half heard, one son is called.
My son! my son! Alas! I am so old!
May he not glad my eyes the little space
Before I go? How can I live, Seth gone?
And Amos by himself, how can he live?
Perchance I erred in leaving thus my tribe.
Were ours the ways of others, woman's love
Were his, and children round his knees ere long.
But now, if Seth is taken, when I go
Goes all companionship of like with like,
And he be but the spectre of a man
Wandering amid his flocks, or sink at last
Into a waiter on the tents of Cain.
Amos—for my heart tells me Seth must go—
And I have asked for counsel of the Lord,
And had no answer—nothing but the doom,
'Who first shall mount the hill!'
                         The doom?   The call:
I may not think it doom: ' He is the Lord's.'
Alas! have I not sinned to call it doom,

Even in thought?—I to whom God hath given,
Such blessed glimmerings of eternal light
That all things fade I see. My son! my son!
If the Lord takes thee, blessed be the Lord,
Who takes but what He gives, and takes to give.

> [*After a pause.*

To gaze on beauty evermore! Why now
It is a joy to my old eyes to watch
The light play of His sunshine through the green
Around me as I sit, to mark far off
The glow on the unclouded plain—a joy
To think of all the goodness I have known
And know—a joy to dream of her I loved
Deepest of all, and strengthening day by day.
Then what must his be who can gaze
On beauty's source, eternal, increate—
On goodness in its essence, and on love!
Love! ——

> Ha! That was a voice! They come—he
comes—
And there a head! Now out on my dull sight!
Where is it? where?   Alas! I fix it not.
A sudden faintness chills my sickening heart,
All things reel from me—pathway, sunshine, trees—
Reel into cloud. 'The first that mounts the hill!'
O God, whichever comes, Thy will be done!

Enter SETH.

SETH.

Father! Good Heavens! Father!

SALEPH.

                  Not ill, but faint.
So let me lean upon thee. Where is Amos?

SETH.

He looks after the mules. He will be here
Just now. You might have seen him as he passed.

SALEPH.

Passed where? where did he pass?

SETH.

                  Why, by the path
Yonder. You look so scared, and are so pale—
We must not leave you by yourself again.

SALEPH.

'Tis but a nothing, that will soon be gone.
This breeze is life—the blessed breath of life.
If Adam had not sinned, we all had lived.
And you both came together up the hill?

SETH.

Oh yes, together till the two paths separate.

SALEPH.

And then ?

SETH.

Well, then we took our different ways.
But you are ill; you look so pale and haggard.

SALEPH.

Not ill.   And so thou knowest not which was first ?

SETH.

I did not heed : the mules were brisk just then
Winding for home, else were my straighter steps
The shorter too.   You might have seen from this.

SALEPH.

Ah! yes, I might have seen from this.   We might
See all things, but God wills it not.   And thou,
How has thy journey sped ?   No ill hath chanced ?

SETH.

No ill.   Yet we have seen strange sights, and first
The daughter of their king.   We killed her dog,
And thus became good friends.   We found she was
The daughter of the king.

SALEPH.

And she was fair ?

SETH.

Nay, dark, more dark than fair, with mocking tongue,
And strength and quickness wondrous in a girl.
She leaped a chasm where I could scarcely follow.

SALEPH.

What, in the town?

SETH.

              No, on the mountain-side
Where she was hunting. When a storm came on
Both she and I took shelter in a cave.

SALEPH.

And she was handsome?

SETH.

             Handsome? Well, perhaps so;
I did not mark, there were such curious things.

SALEPH.

How curious?

SETH.

             Horrible! In a deep nook
Above a cleft where a great river poured,
In a strange cave, a girl lay starved to death.
It is their punishment for those who'd save
Their sons.

SALEPH.

How long, O Lord, how long? And she,
How she must shudder at the sight!

SETH.

                              She shudder!
Unless a jibe's a shudder.   Here comes Amos.

Enter AMOS.

Nay look not thus, brother: he's better now.

SALEPH.

Ay, better, Amos, better far, quite strong.
The old man's heart was weary for his sons.
Now they have come it will grow light once more.
Saw you again the maid of whom you speak?

SETH.

Ay: in the city, when our work was done,
Our idle steps had led us to a space,
A central space, with a great earthen mound,
Where shooters practised with their bows. One man,
A grizzly-bearded man, had beaten all,
Women and men—for there were women there
Who strove—young girls arrayed in manly guise—
Until a cry went up, a shrilly cry,

Of ' Arvah ! Arvah !' and we saw our guide
Drawing her long bow to the ear, and lo
An arrow quivered in the very mark.
Another and another, quick as words.
While all the women shouted till I thought
My ears were pierced, and straight a little girl—
A little child girl I had seen before,
Who gave the chain of gold that you have now—
Ran out and laid a green crown on her head,
And all were mad with joy.

AMOS.

Not all.   I heard
No hoarser note.   The men were mute, and some
Whispered, with savage glances.

SALEPH.

Is it so ?
I ever knew such should be in the end.
Sooner or later, when the cup was full,
Nature must win.

AMOS.

Ay, win, that was her word—
' Better to win than die.'

SETH.

And then the girls,
The armed girls, raised her upon a shield,

While all the place was glittering with their spears.
We heard the shouts still as our laden mules
Passed out the city gates.

AMOS.
Not all the place—
Less than a third of it—slight girls. I saw
The younger men half smile as they looked on;
But all the elders and the horrid crowd
Of bloated women glared in silent rage.
Most terrible is hate in human eyes.

SALEPH.
Such hate is homage paid by vice to virtue.

SETH.
Virtue? Can virtue be in the accursed?

SALEPH.
My son, God loves all who will let Him love.
Perchance those most to whom least has been given,
When all that's given is prized.   If these young girls
Will strive till death against the cruel wrong
Thus done to nature and to nature's God
In them and such as them, are they not His?
'Twere well for us were we as true.

SETH.
And yet
They come of Cain.

SALEPH.

> And we of Eve, who sinned
> Deeper perchance than Cain, sinning the first.
> God ruins no man for another's sin,
> Being ever just and merciful, then most
> When understood the least ; though here I err
> As if there were degrees of goodness in Him,
> Who in all things and each is still most good,
> And can be nothing but most good.   This girl
> May be Heaven's chosen instrument.

AMOS.

> Alone,
> With her strange skill and strength, few were her
>   match.
> But when I looked upon her girlish train,
> And then on the huge shoulders and bare arms
> Around me as I stood—arms whose great curves
> Seemed hardened into rocks by age and toil—
> I felt a struggle must have issue such
> As with such men we scarce may think upon.

SETH.

> Yet thinking on what we may scarce think on,
> Our Amos here hath grown the dreariest man
> From this to the great plains of father Seth.
> Scarce one word spoke he on our homeward way,

And now has not one word to speak of home.
How are the young lambs, father, since we left?
The rain-storm must have served the softer grass.

SALEPH.

They were all safe when I unbarred the fold
At sunrise, though some limped as if they missed
The shepherd's care.   The dogs have never strayed,
Feeling twice charged.   Go see with thine own eyes.
Amos and I will tarry here a while.

SETH.

Thanks, father: then I go.   Perchance your voice
Will charm this melancholy wight of ours,
And make him better company ere night.

[Exit SETH.

SALEPH.

How gay he is!

AMOS.

Most gay; soon we shall hear
The welcome of his dogs barking him home.

SALEPH.

So gay, so good, how he must love his life!

AMOS.

You sigh; he loves it not too much.

SALEPH.

Thy meaning.

AMOS.

I've seen him risk it for risk's sake ; yet that
I mean not, such being rather love of life
That makes a pleasure of the gain.   Seth loves his
As good that should for greater good be given,
As good that of itself still tends to less,
But first as good free-gained which he who gives
Lends to the Lord.   He dreams of Paradise,
And of the mystic portal none may find
Save pure of heart, and he alone can enter
So guarded from the angel's sword of flame
Who'd die to save a sin ; yet even then
Can enter but to die.

SALEPH.

        More things will kill
Than sickness or the sword.   Who enters there
Hears secrets that no man can hear and live,
Withering thenceforth with longings of great joy.

AMOS.

And yet you know and live.

SALEPH.

        I have not been
Within the sacred portal.

AMOS.

But were given
To read the maze that seems unreadable.

SALEPH.

My son, believe, and thou shalt see.   Myself,
In vision or in truth, for which I know not,
Being spent with toil and travel o'er the waste
And all the fiery flashes of the noon,
Beheld the walls that gird the garden round.
But as I gazed their deep sides turned to dream,
And all things turned to dream, and I was borne
Westward towards the low sun, whose evening glow
Made a red glory round my camel's ears.
Some hours had slipped out of my life, and lo !
A hand unbound my tunic from my throat,
Moistening my parched lips as I lay back faint.
Then first I saw thy mother.

AMOS.

And think you
Those cliffs were in good truth the circling walls
Of the fair garden where our father woke ?

SALEPH.

So deemed I, yet had toiled and fasted long.
For days all thought was prayer ; for days the sun

Glowed like a brazen furnace in the sky.
It may be that their show was but some flaw
In my distempered brain.

AMOS.

>   'Tis sure the garden

Does stand?

SALEPH.

>   Most sure.   I've heard our kinsman Enoch

Dwells there in peace.

AMOS.

>   And yet you said no man

Could enter it and live.

SALEPH.

>   I meant no man

Who sought the place of his own will.   Enoch
The Lord who took him guards for some great end.

AMOS.

And think you that the chosen ones
Who enter read the mysteries of pain
That turn this fair world sometimes to a hell,
Tracing the perfect purpose through them all?

SALEPH.

Not all, my son; I doubt that human mind
Can fathom all, but much; and he learns much
Who seeks in all things but to do God's will;

Who strives to find in all things His great love ;
And most who wills to take a fellow's pain,
To give God joy, and man.

AMOS.

         Poor insect lives,
How can we give a joy to the high God ?

SALEPH.

He loves us, and who loves hath joy in love,
And thoughts and deeds of love from those they love.

AMOS.

Alas ! could we but feel as sure of this
As we are sure of that we see and taste.
And yet it should be true if human hearts
Are made for truth, as hand to grasp and eye
To see, for it alone can fill their longings.
But now I crave a favour. I know not
What you will think of it, it is so strange.
I wish to be alone a day or two
In the deep woods.   Ask not my purpose, father ;
I scarce have purpose that would clothe in words;
Yet even I might hear the voice of God.

SALEPH.

It seems but yesterday thou wert a child,
A gentle child, and now—well, be it so.

Thy mother trained thee first with little steps ;
A yard, then two, and so her hand, then three.
Yes, go my son, in three days' time return.
Return; the time will come, and soon, thou'd fain
Have such return.   I blame thee not, Amos.
There, let me lean on thee, and we'll go home,
And tell me as we go of that brave girl,
That child of a bad race that seems so good.
Nay, stumble not, it shakes me painfully ;
Yet once I, too, was young.

SCENE II.

*A wooded glade in the mountains over the city of Cain. A
fire burning.*

ARVAH and HEVIRAH.

ARVAH.

A famous cook !
For half a life I have not dined so well ;
And thou, how likest thou the sauce, Hevirah ?

HEVIRAH.

Poor stupid cook, that Arvah likes to puzzle !
Prithee, what sauce ?

ARVAH.

Why liberty, my girl ;
The chainless monntain air ; the honest toil
That brought good nature's blessing to the feast.

HEVIRAH.

It was so pretty with its golden neck,
Despite thy arrow in its breast.   I thought
I ne'er saw bird so beautiful.

ARVAH.

Tut, child !
When those small hands had plucked the feathery
   gold,
And from that rod it had turned round and round
Until the fragrance nearly starved us both,
'Twas three times beautiful.   When I am king
Thou shalt be prince of spits.

HEVIRAH.

I humbly thank
Thy gracious kingship, and make bold to ask—
Having a promise that my prayer be heard
Now that the bones are picked—why are we here ?

ARVAH.

Thou vexing thing ! still harping on that theme.
Thou, too, wert sick of dull white walls and beards

See how the squirrels glide in agile play
Through all the evening freshness of the trees ;
Beneath, the lambs are racing down yon slope
In gay companionship of like with like.
Here all young things are glad ; we too, my sister.

HEVIRAH.

And here how can we live ?

ARVAH.

As now.　My bow
Shall strike the quarry for our daily meal,
My axe cut down the wood that lights our fire;
A little tiresome cook will do the rest,
Gathering the rotten windfalls, too, by times ;
And when each heavy eyelid droops at last
Upon the leafy wonder of the scene,
Will lay her head by Arvah's side and sleep.

HEVIRAH.

Or on her Arvah's heart, as thus ; so lean
Thy hand upon my head.　And now put by
This untrue mood and tell me all, my sister.

ARVAH.

Thou little wise wise wench !—what is to tell ?

HEVIRAH.

What made thy brow so like our sculptured god's—
It is a face I dread—when late last night
I hailed thee on the roof?—why did thy form
So quiver in my clasp?   Thou then didst promise
That I should know ere long.

ARVAH.

And so thou shalt.
Ere long those young things shall be sick, or old,
Or dead.

HEVIRAH.

But now they know not they must die.
Or distance can half hide the horror.   I
Do know that Arvah's smile is but a mask,
And long to gaze upon the face I love.

ARVAH.

All smiles are masks, or are like his who sits
Each day beside our gate—the idiot
Who toys with his own sores—so now would I
A little while ; or rather as the things
That see no future and are merry, I
Would glad me on this summer night.   And yet
As thou wilt have it, let it be.   Sister,
Resting last eve upon my couch, I heard
My own name muttered in our father's chamber,
And listening, knew the voice of the chief sage.

I long have seen there were who loved me not,
Who deem, forsooth, I stir up mutiny,
Making the younger girls ape mannish ways,
And loathe the customs of our race.   Strong Zoar
Had asked me of the king as wife ; that, too,
I knew—-his thousandth wife all counted.   Still
I feared not, trusting much myself and some
His love—my father's love.   But listen, sister :
Last night I heard their plot—my father's plot.
There is some cursed herb—or so they think—
That hath as property to rob the mind
Of its due strength and mastery.   This I—
The same being mingled with my food—should eat,
And in the after palsy of the will,
Ere yet the fumes had passed, do their behests,
Thus giving brave example to the rest.
By Cain, a stout man, Zoar !   He safer far
Had laid his unarmed hand on panther's crest,
Than tried such jest on Arvah.

HEVIRAH.
                                    And you fly ?
ARVAH.
Why, what a world of wonder's in that tone !

HEVIRAH.
You leave the hearts that love you to their fate—
The chosen ones, that would have died for you.
You mock me still, my sister !

ARVAH.

Do I mock?

Why look around you.   We are here—we two.

HEVIRAH.

Yes, you are here; therefore I know you mock.

ARVAH.

My little conscience, if I do the base,
I see the right or 'tis no fault of thine.
What would you have?

HEVIRAH.

Have you yourself in life
Or death—not like the fickle beasts that play,
And die, and leave no thought.

ARVAH.

None leave a thought;
Nothing but bones and putrid flesh.

HEVIRAH.

'Tis false!

I am a child and find not words for much,
And cannot cope with you; but this I *feel*,
Who lives a life that's good and brave and true,
Leaves something besides bones.

ARVAH.

Or dies a death.

HEVIRAH.

Or dies a death! O Arvah! let us die
If so it must be. Let all die together.

ARVAH.

Then all were lost indeed. Were I to die
It were my joy to think that you would live,
And I live in your thoughts. My little one,
You would still love me were I dead? There, there,
I know you would. Then ever think of this
Fair night we sat together in the trees,
And know I would not be the thing I played
For all we feign the cruel gods to be.

HEVIRAH.

I knew you mocked me. Why, then, are we here?

ARVAH.

I dared not stay knowing their plot, nor dared
To show my knowledge, and thus challenge all
So unprepared. This is the middle course,
And gives me time for thought, perchance for action.
Often before I thus have sought the woods—
The pleasant summer woods—the things I love,
And thee.

HEVIRAH.

I do remember 'twas a jest
That Arvah went alone, but that her dogs
Might tell strange tales if dogs could use their
    tongues.

ARVAH.

And you believed their trash ?

HEVIRAH.

                Not I ; I deemed
It but the foolishness of empty heads.
I had not given then a chain of gold,
Nor heard of certain meetings on the hills,
Else had I been less sure.

ARVAH.

                You little rogue !
I thought you were too wise to chatter thus.
Now lie you on that tufted moss and sleep.
I wish we had our dogs.   I had no heart
To take them since the faithfullest was gone.
But rest secure, for I will watch the while.
                [*After a pause.*
She sleeps already ; toil has done its work.
Was I so right to make her speak those words ?
Ere long, when all is done, she'll think of them,
And thinking, grieve—it may be she will grieve

When all is done!   Things can have but one end.
We are outmatched—a hundred times outmatched.
Eastward the young man pointed to their home,
And eastward still the constant track has turned.
I know their father will befriend the child
In that wild home; then I'll return alone—
I wonder will they stand to me—poor girls!.
'Tis hard to meet strong men in battle—I
Am strong, therefore I feel it not, nor care
To live, therefore I fear it not; but they—
Well, time will tell; if all things come to worst,
I die true to myself; that's much; and more,
True to my image in the heart I love.

> [*After a pause.*

We scarce can miss the trail, the laden mules
Have made so deep a track. 'Twas strange he
   wore not
The chain of gold; it would have held his knife,
And graced his broad chest well.   The other one
Is not so tall, but hath the stronger brow,
Strong with a gentle soberness of strength.
The child will love him soon with all her heart,
And so forget poor Arvah.   Nay, not so—
I must not wrong my darling—how she sleeps,
Calm as an infant on the mother's breast—
A little infant with its small clasped hands;
None such will ever lie on mine.   Tut, fool!

Thou hast foresworn thy sex ; thy babes are spears,
Sword, bow, and all the implements of death.
Ah ! no, no, no. 'Tis for my babes I fight,
My little tiny boys that they would kill—
My rosy plunging boys. I see them now,
Fat chubby things that cling around my steps.
Gods ! Are there gods that love the blood of such ?
Then thus I spit upon their power—defy them—
Cry shame upon them, loathe them, hate and scorn—
Could their dread Moloch, that they sculpture fair,
Now rise before me in his cruel strength,
I'd taunt, spurn, execrate, while words were mine.
But this is foolishness—there is no god—
Nothing so wicked on the earth as man,
Man that hath good and evil in his choice,
And would be happy if he chose the good.
If every human thing were like that child,
Or like the youths I seek and their old father,
Such as they picture him—'twere well to live.
But now—well now, perhaps, 'tis well to die—
To die !—alas to feel, see, hear no more,
To be for ever nothing—one great void—
Nay nothing great, but just a simple void.
The empty air I grasp thus in my hand
Holds millions such as I am soon to be ;
I that now think and love. And is this all ?
Is all that will remain of me the dream,

The passing dream, in one heart soon to fade?
Strange how I shudder at the thought.   Nothing—
Is it not better, then, to live?—to live
As I have dreamed these last long days—peaceful
And happy in some hut—I and Hevirah,
Tending the old man in his gracious age—
And so leave all things to their fate, deserting
The girls that I have made.   No, not if years
As numberless as is the dust I tread
In all its separate grains, were mine, and joys
Through each without a pain!   I could not do it.
It does not tempt me, for I feel I could not.
But why?   Surely a joyous life outweighs a void.
There is no reason in it.   Is there none?
She would not love me if I were so base,
I could not love myself were I so base:
But can I love myself when I am dead,
And can I know she loves me when I am dead?
Oh, gentle child, how I do love thy love!
It is my guide, my star, my all—Hevirah,
The little wise wise thing that I have nursed.
Were I to dream a God it were like thee,
As pure, as brave, as gentle, and as true:
Some one to counsel death when I should die
And counselling to long to die with me!
Ah if such God there were, how I could pray!
But if such God there were, He would be strong,

And would not die Himself or let me die.
And then I could not love Him like the child;
If now I die, I die to be myself,
To keep my faith unbroken and my life
Pure as it has been; that the thought of me
May rest unspotted on the heart I love,
Therefore I die.   And now to sell my life
As dearly as I can.   If he were with us
Who stayed alone the crowd the day the woman
Stole through the city wall, I'd still have hope.
How beautiful he looked! undaunted, bright,
The black curls crisping round his youthful brow,
Fairer than mine; and yet a king of men
I scarce could find it in my heart to play—
                    Great Cain, what now!

HEVIRAH (*awakening*).
Arvah! the light! O Arvah!

ARVAH.
Fear not, fear not; my hand is round you, fear not;
It is the fire mountain; gods, what a flame!.

HEVIRAH.
A god is rising in his wrath: Moloch!

ARVAH.
How the earth shakes! Our mother's mighty breast
Is quivering with her throes; it rises still.

HEVIRAH.

O Arvah, let us hide behind the rocks!

ARVAH.

Hush; none can hide from Nature; rocks may gape.
How the great light makes all shine luridly.

HEVIRAH.

I cannot look; it is too terrible.
O Arvah, let us hide!

ARVAH.

        Fear not, fear not!
Strangely the palely lightnings flash on either side
From out a central red—a tower of fire.

HEVIRAH.

I dare not look.   Alas! that dreadful noise,
Like many thunders muffled in the ground!

ARVAH.

There's not a stone upon the mountain side
But shines.   The thin rills show like liquid gleams;
I see the flatness of our roofs below,
And almost hear the wakened sleepers cry.

HEVIRAH.

'Twere terrible if the great flame should fall
Upon the city.

ARVAH.

Hear how the scared birds
Scream through the trees ! The arched boughs o'er-
    head
Glow as if lit by torches, the great sky
Like flame on burnished shield.

HEVIRAH.

But the cloud ! the cloud !

ARVAH.

The topmost flame is hid beneath its folds,
Deep murky folds that slowly widening fall,
Yet glimmers luridly in sudden glimpses,
Like face of demon glaring through their horror.

HEVIRAH.

It is a god that threatens thus the city.

ARVAH.

Then fire must be a god. But hark ! that sound,
That sudden sharper sound, as strength that bursts,
And see the quick sparks rise through all the sky.

HEVIRAH.

Like the red circlings of a fiery plume
Half hid in the deep cloud. Hush ! what was that ?

F

ARVAH.

The falling of great stones upon the trees—
The sparks were burning masses. Now indeed
'Tis time to fly. Beneath yon arching trunk
Is shelter.

SCENE III.

Another part of the same wood.

AMOS.

Both are asleep at last. Long time the child
Lay wakeful in her fear; and when a light
Would flicker through the trees, marking the flame
Still fitful on the mountain-top, started;
And then were murmurs of soft words, until
At last she slept. The other strove to watch,
Lest beasts might steal upon them slumbering.
I know she strove, even as I watch now,
And once in the awakening glow I saw
Her face as she bent o'er the sleeper. Mother,
My mother, was it thus you looked on me
In those old misty times I almost see
On the year's verge—dim verge?

                     Ha! there again!
Again the glimmer brightening all the trees,

But each less vivid now. Does God thus threaten
The wicked ones below—in mercy threaten?
Or is it Nature's law in blindest round,
Working its brute will on the affrighted earth,
That makes the night thus fearful? Nature's law?
The law of Nature is the law of God ;
Her rules His rules, by Him still chosen and framed ;
So speaks my father, and then hints at more ;
Hints that these laws fixed-seeming are not fixed,
But that all brute things, from the glorious sun
To the soft dust-grain flitting down the wind,
Obey the Will that rules all things but man,
And stranger still, rules each of us for each.
I cannot fathom it, nor yet deny.
I know my free will me, and knowing dread,
But know no more ; all else is cloud. If God
Is bound by His own laws and others' thoughts,
Why should I pray? All things must take their
    course,
And yet I pray ; my father prays, and finds
His prayers are granted. All is cloud. If God
Were but His laws, or even bound by them,
Why should we love Him as He bids us love,
Loving all things that happen as His will—
Pain, pleasure, and the rest ; finding in each
The thoughtful love that's ever fixed on one,
And that one each own separate self.

This is to love God as my father loves.
Surely a great love, worthy man's great heart,
The heart that feels itself a universe,
Not a mere speck on an united earth.
But is this pride, the sin that He most hates ?
Nay, rather gratitude, that owns the gift
And loves the Maker more in His great gift,
And worships in each brother the same gift.
Pride ! why, 'tis rather true humility,
If it be true, for truth cannot be pride,
But must for ever humble us who know
That we have little from ourselves but sin.
Oh God, to think that man that thou has framed
So noble and so strong, and some so fair—
So fair beyond all things that are most fair—
As those two sleepers are, can rend thy laws,
Even the law that makes us most like Thee.
Well may the fire threaten, yet not them ;
It did not threaten them.   Strange, she is here,
And I—I scarcely dreamed she might be here.
How that weird hope thrills through my inmost soul,
She here and I.   Is this that destiny
That rules our acts in an accord mysterious
Beyond all human thought with our own wills ?
If so it be, O God if so it be,
Thine be the praise for all the rapture mine !
Here on our trail, or almost on our trail,

It well may be she seeks our father's hut
As refuge from the danger threatening,
She and her sister.   How the old man's heart
Would gladden at their coming, feeling youth
Renewed in their sweet faces even while
His words would breathe new faith, new hope, new
   love
Through all their darkened lives.   I see them now,
The three sitting beside the porch at eve,
As Seth and I come from our daily toil,
Or in the autumn morns binding the sheaves,
The dewy sheaves that glisten as they bind.
If this be ours, O then indeed my life
Were but too short for gratitude ; my days
And nights, waking, shall be one hymn of praise.
Yea, at the bare imagining, I feel
How Seth can long to die for God being good,
To die for Him because He is so good.
But surely we can please Him without death ;
To die is not His only law.   Death is
A punishment, not law.   In gentle love,
In meekness that would feel rather than hurt,
In constant care to guard another's life,
Surely the path to God may be in these ;
Yet over all there is the dread of death,
And over all the mystery of pain—
The one great riddle none can solve but he.

So says our father, who would give his life
To give God joy and man.   Am I so brave ?
Alas, I know not ; but until I know
I'll do what little good I can, though little,
And take what joys I can, leaving the rest
To destiny.

Act III.

SCENE 1.

The grove before Saleph's cottage.

SALEPH and SETH.

SETH.

Above the hills a strange and sudden light
Made the west grow all red. I would our Amos
Were back.

SALEPH.

    It may be that the forest burned
Beyond the mountains.

SETH.

        Half an hour it lasted,
Then grew more dim ; but all the while a sound,
A low dull echoing of distant sound,
Shook the tranced air. I deem not such the show,
The genial show, of Nature.

SALEPH.

      Yet has she horrors,
Sore-striving Nature that has fallen with man ;
Witness the thunder and the sudden flash
That quivers through men's hearts as through the
  air.

SETH.

'Tis true Nature can smite ; but tell me, father,
Had Eve alone been sinner, what had chanced ?

SALEPH.

God knows, my son, not I.

SETH.

      Had I been Adam
When I had known her and the serpent's crime,
I would have waited for the Lord when next
He walked, and asked to share, as she was woman,
The punishment, though not the sin.   It may be
He is so good He then had pardoned both.
Are you quite sure the Garden stands till now
Where once it stood ?

SALEPH.

    Most certainly it stands.

SETH.

Then why may not all find the sacred gate,
And watch the sword of flame ?

SALEPH.

                                   Because the Lord
Hath need of loving trust and acts love-born,
Not bred of fear alone.   Were the stern walls
And sin's dread penalty by all men seen,
Plain selfish fear would broaden virtue's path
For baser wills.   It is not thus, my son ;
The fear that is of justice is of God,
The great foundation-stone of holy life ;
But fear alone saves not, therefore the vision
And the plain proofs of God's primeval ways
With man, may be but guerdon of the end.

SETH.

But if the walls stand, why cannot all find them ?

SALEPH.

Because the Lord so wills.   On every side
Now flames the desert and the burning sun
Whose arid lustres flashing on dazed eyes
May well be typed in sword angelic.   O'er the waste
Broad, level, trackless shimmering still with heat,
No man can steer the fated course but he
Whom heaven hath chosen.   So in things natural,
Of which plain order angel-guarded Eden
Scarce is, men roam on all sides of a truth
That found at last, seems in the common path

To stand.   While of the subtler essences
More subtle as more strong, that round us flit,
Proved to experience though ungrasped by sense,
We form no dream that in its wildest mood
Is not within the facts.   I've heard of men
Who lived a ghostly age in some short seconds;
Then may not worlds of supernatural space
Be grasped in the close span our arms can hold,
And so with Paradise ?

SETH.

I like better
The other thought, that makes the real garden,
With real shubs and trees and fruits and flowers,
Ready to welcome him whom God shall lead
Across the sands.   Without a camel, father,
None may essay the quest?

SALEPH.

Surely, yet that
Is small part of the cost.

SETH.

I know, I know;
I saw a group once in the streets of Cain;
Great hunchback things, like rugged mountain-sides,
That bent to take their burdens patiently.
There are strange sights in those same sun-burned
    streets.

Methought last night o'er them the warning flamed
The deepest glare, reddened the central range;
And there this morn a cloud, or such it seemed,
Confused the midmost summits.   From the rise
Where the paths separate we see their forms
Bounding the distant plain.   I'll steal a look.
Perhaps our Amos comes.

[*Exit* SETH.

SALEPH.

My son! my son!
E'en now his bold frank heart has almost grasped
The mystery of mysteries!   The thought
So terrible in its unsounded depths
That the scared word may well fly from it ever
And the scared mind doubt its own imaging;
And yet so beautiful, the wondrous lines
Once traced, for good or ill last evermore.
He would have shared the pain, though not the sin.
I do not grudge thee to the Lord, Seth, Seth!
My son!

Re-enter SETH.

SETH.

O, father, even now at hand
The maid whose dog we slew, and the young child,
Face hitherward among the trees; she armed
With sword and bow, but other escort none.

SALEPH.

It may be that they seek for shelter.   Son,
Go forth and make them welcome to our state
Thus lowly as it is.   Thine arm; I'll rise,
And greet them standing.   [*Exit* SETH.
                    Strange !   Thus are we moved
Like puppets o'er the unconscious earth, willing
Yet impotent in act almost as it,
Our wills are bounded by the willing; beyond
All powerless.   Amos gone, and lo, she comes,
The daughter of the race of Cain, but chaste
And good and ——

Enter SETH, ARVAH and HEVIRAH.

                    Maidens, you are welcome both,
Whose strange feet seek this scarcely trodden land,
Strange and yet not unknown to us and ours.
If we can tempt your stay in this our rude haunt,
We'll welcome you with hearts rather than words,
Craving your pardon for our common speech,
Who would be courteous to all men as kings.

ARVAH.

Being in very truth most kingly thus ;
I pray you, sir, you will not judge us harshly ;
If to your reverend eyes most keen as pure

We seem to lack somewhat of modesty,
Thus venturing unasked and lone so far,
We plead, my sister and myself, sore stress
Of circumstance.

SALEPH.

Who plead for that gives joy
And honour to their judges plead not in truth,
But clothe the gifts they bring with noblest show
Of pleading.   Queens and daughters, you are wel-
    come.
When my hair was as his, I too have mixed
With such as you; not kings—Seth has no kings—
But such in gentle nurture and humility.

SETH.

Gentle!   You did not see her fly at Amos
For her dead dog.   Spare me such gentleness!

ARVAH.

'Twas you were gentle, sir; it is most true,
Your pleading to get out was quite bewitching.

SETH.

Jibing already?   Well well, jeer away;
You've earned the right by being thus, good comrade.

ARVAH.

Nay, then, I claim a comrade's right to blow
For blow, 'twere stupid fencing else with word

Or stick.   But we have kept your father standing.
May I not help you, sir?

SALEPH.

I thank thee much.
Standing I feel a tower, an old and bent one,
That makes my own head giddy with its height.
Thank thee again ; if that I hear be true,
The arm I lean on is no weak one either.

HEVIRAH.

In all the streets of Cain there is none like it
For sword or bow.

ARVAH.

I prithee, sister, peace,
Else this huge man will force a quarrel straightway
To prove himself unmatched.

SALEPH.

A blow well aimed.
If but thy arrow hit the mark as truly,
Thou art a warrior worthy of his might.

HEVIRAH.

She never misses, and once killed a lion.

ARVAH.

Thou little babbler! Sir, I pray you excuse
This over-forward love that magnifies

Her own big sister's mole-hills into mountains.
But in good truth we passed this morn a panther
Hard by our last night's resting-place, fresh slain.
The grinning horror of its teeth against
The froth-stained earth haunts me all day.   Around
Footsteps of man in earnest struggle tracked,
And blood, and blow deep dinted on the brain,
Told of how hard the tawny robber died.
It were no tame awakening in his grip,
Believe me, sirs. I speak who slept too nigh,
I and the child.   I wonder had your giantship
Been quite as good at need.

SETH.

                    I would not ask
Better than trial. I can say no more.

ABVAH.

And have said that so well we need no more.
In very truth quick words ill suit such hour ;
How pleasantly the amber-tinted light
Plays hide and seek through all the rippling trees,
Making each leaf on ivied trunk vibrate
Half cloud, half sunshine. Who would live in dens
Stone-built by men, when these wide palaces,
With Nature's festive hangings ever clad,
Are pillared for us thus ?

SETH.

That's beautiful!
And yet methinks when winter rains pour down
Those same green trunks, 'twere pleasant to have roof
Over one's head.

ARVAH.

O most inconsequent.
He longs for lion's claws who fears the rain.

SETH.

Not so; he loves to ward off rain with thatch
Who'd stay your other friend another way.

ARVAH.

Being quite as easy, too !

SETH.

Nay, easier.
It takes a man to stretch a roof.   I've heard
Of girl that killed a lion.

ARVAH.

Now, by Cain,
That girl ne'er boasted what she did ; still less
That which she might, could, would do.

HEVIRAH.

                        Having ever

A little sister by her side, you know,

To magnify her mole-hills into mountains.

ARVAH.

What! two to one, then I shall quit the field.

But of these roofs; if you must have a roof,

I'd love one nestling in a forest glade,

Where the young sun dries tangled roses' tears,

Waking the drowsy sleepers with the cheer

Of morning gladness.

SETH.

                  Such a one is ours.

Not thrice a hundred paces hence, with wing

Facing the east above a gardened slope,

A gentle slope where summer corn waves.

You two must henceforth share it with my father;

Amos and I will watch outside.

ARVAH.

                        Nay, I

Should take my turn, for I am warrior too.

Have you much work to do upon your fields?

SALEPH.

But little now, my daughter; toil is over.

Now is the summer sabbath of the year

                  * G

When man rests while the bounteous harvests grow.
(*To Seth*) Wilt thou not seek again the outer trees?
Perchance thy brother comes.

SETH.

Oh, he comes not;
He's mooning it quite to his heart's content
Somewhere about the woods.

ARVAH.

Nay, sunning it.
But woods, what woods? The woods follow the moun-
        tains,
Save these.

SETH.

And thither he.   I marked his form
Descending on the plain from whence you came.

SALEPH.

He will be back ere night; and then to-morrow,
If you will hearken to an old man's prayer,
Our work shall be to build another wing
For certain well-timed guests.

SETH.

A famous plan.
Amos and I can rear the walls while they
O'erlook the dogs that guard the straving flock.

ARVAH.

For this kind thought, O father, and thou, friend,
Receive what we can give—our thanks. Would that
The joy you offer it were mine to take;
The very dream of it makes life more sweet,
Not as to prisoned wretch who thirsts and sees
The water through his bars, but as they joy
Who look upon a glorious sunset scene,
Happy they know not why.

SETH.

              Better to thirst,
And break the bars and drink.

SALEPH.

               Not so, my son.
Who drinks will thirst again; but who hath joy
In beauty, peace, and goodness for themselves,
Hath that makes glad for evermore.

SETH.

                Give me
The cool draught; it is worth a dozen sunsets.

SALEPH.

Son, let not daughter of the stranger speak
More like a child of God than thou.

SETH.
                   Your pardon.
I have offended, that I know, but how?
The lambkins of my flock are wise as I.

ARVAH.
We'll beg for you ; and yet you touched a sore point
With the wee minstrel here who hath her song,
Her special song, about the suuset hour.

SALEPH.
Ha! is it so?   I've heard the sons of Caiu
Were much renowned for music ; yet heard too—
It matters not ; with this sweet singer here
We well may know the gift is turned to good.
I pray thee glad us with thy art, my child.

HEVIRAH
I have no harp.

ARVAH.
           Yet sing the song I spoke of.

HEVIRAH.
'Tis but a childish one.

(*She sings.*)

    The sun goes down on the evening land,
    Where the gates of his far-off palace stand ;
    Land bright with the rays that scorch not there,
    Gates golden with glory that is not glare.

O Sun! O Sun! in that palace high,
What beauty of joy must glad the eye.
O Sun! O Sun! take me to see
Me and my comrades two and three.

'My child,' 'tis his voice, 'I have toiled the day,
Warming and lighting and bright alway,
Ere yet I sink down in the happy West,
Ere yet these golden gates are blest.'

So we, O friends, so we must move,
Striving and helping and bright with love,
Until the heat of the day be past,
Until we melt into joy at last.

HEVIRAH.

Who stands yonder amid the trees, listening?

SALEPH and SETH.

Amos!

SCENE II.

In front of Saleph's cottage.

SETH and AMOS.

SETH

The light is out.   They sleep.

AMOS.

Or try to sleep.   Sleep comes not at the will.
Oft when we need rest more, we rest the least;

The over-quickened brain whirls on and on
With fevered impetus of its own thought,
And mocks the effort to be calm.

SETH.

                  But they
Are now in peace ; then wherefore should they
    wake ?

AMOS.

In peace !   Think you the maiden means to tarry
Beneath our father's roof ?

SETH.

             And wherefore not ?

AMOS

 Ere yon bright moon hath lost its circle quite,
She goes.

SETH.

    Goes where ?

AMOS.

              It may be to her death.
Uutil to-night I hoped, but hope no more.
Think you I met her here by chance ?   Not so.
Ere sundown yester eve I struck their trail—
Our trail—and guessed that they faced hitherward.

SETH.

Their trail ? Then it was you that killed the panther ?

AMOS.

It was.

SETH.

Well done!   Why not have told us of it?

AMOS.

I tell you now; but for our love be silent!

SETH.

And wherefore?

AMOS.

She might think it hard I spied
Upon her slumber thus.

SETH.

Now, in good truth,
The panther were the sorer spy.   I tell you,
With nothing but your staff, 'twas a grand feat.
How came he on?   You waited till he sprang—
So—did you not?—then threw him back and struck;
Come in, and tell my father.

AMOS.

Hush! Seth, hush!
Your words will wake the sleepers if they sleep.
You must not tell my father; tell no one.

SETH.

Tell no one?   Why, if I had killed the brute,
I'd talk of it for a week.   Well, well, good night;
Since you won't come I'll leave you to your dreams.
I must go sleep.   [*Exit* SETH.

AMOS.

                Good night, I shall not wake you.
How like a giant of old times he stalks
Away amid the trees.   If she must go,
His arm were worth a hundred.   I can see him
Cutting and carving, with that sword he loves,
Amid their grey beards in the soddened street,
The red dust-soddened street.   Is it not strange
That such a thought can fire the blood?—to kill,
To make God's suffering image writhe, it may be
With throes none can conceive who hath not felt,
Until they thrust the sinful spirit forth
From the poor clay it loves.   Can this be glorious?

(*Re-enter* SETH.)

SETH.

Come Amos, come along!   Why do you stay here
Moping about the door—a second night, too;
You'll wake me when you come—that's the worst
    of it.

AMOS.

Then I'll not go at all ; a bank of moss,
Here, anywhere, will suit me just as well
As that snug lair you vaunt so, such fair night
As this.

SETH.

Why, was there ever such a fool!

[*Exit* SETH.

AMOS.

There is no glory in thus slaying men ;
The glory is in risking to be slain
For worthy end—to save, to right the weak ;
Or, as Seth feels, to serve the God that made us.
He was not at his best to-night, our Seth ;
Far from it, far ; I scarcely knew my brother,
In jest, and jeer, and scornful-seeming laugh ;
Alas ! he could not feel, as I felt then,
That laugh was blasphemy upon the verge
Of death, and death in darkness where she stands.
Scarce dare I sleep, fearing lest horrid jeers
Of bestial men and hideous bloated women
Break on me round her agonising form.
Such dread presage too often comes in dream,
Or rather ghosts of waking thought haunting us.
Of death in darkness.   Hers is not the light
Of everlasting hope, making death beautiful,

And yet she gives her life to save a sin.
The thought was written on the resolute brow
Through all the banter of her words to-night;
Strange that Seth saw it not and showed so ill,
Alas! why should God speak to us and not to her!
Fool! who am I that thus would line His ways,
'He loves those most to whom least has been given,
When all that's given is prized.' So says my father:
And who hath prized his virtue as she prizes,
And yet scarce knows what that is she so prizes?
Her girls will fall from her as chaff. I marked
    them,
And there were those among the older crowd
Looked hell and all its longings. If worst, come—
Ha! what was that? surely I heard a sound.
The door—it opens; as I felt, 'tis she!
She cannot sleep as I. How the pale light
Falls like a halo on her upturned face,
And the thin gold that rings her forehead—sign
Of queenhood. I will play the spy no more:
Maiden, fear not; 'tis I.

ARVAH.

    Thou, and thy brother?

AMOS.

He is not here; he sleeps.

ARVAH.

How bright the moon is!
Her pallid wand chink-thrown upon the wall,
Summoned me forth.   I love to walk at night,
And gaze upon the gentle earth thus veiled.

AMOS.

A lustrous veil.

ARVAH.

In truth, most beautiful.
There is a calm to-night should make all calm.
I cannot think but if bad men would stand
Where we stand now, they were the better for it.

AMOS.

And when the storm would rise should they storm too?

ARVAH.

Why spoil so sweet a lie with your true thought?
'Tis cruel of you.

AMOS.

No lies are sweet; truth is.

ARVAH.

Truth!   Is it sweet to think that yon bright plain,
From all the misty distance to our feet,
Is but one beauteous mockery of rest,
Where life still preys on life, and calm is truce

At best ?   I looked to it for peace, and you
Have spoiled all.

AMOS.

I ?—no truth ?

ARVAH.

I had forgotten ;

Forgetfulness is joy—our only joy.

AMOS.

Nay, rather knowledge, if we knew but all things.

ARVAH.

The bitter joy that knows all things are sham,
And finds in very dreariness pale comfort.

AMOS.

Not so : there are most real goods—truth, courage,
Fidelity.

ARVAH.

The lioness is brave,

The noble dog most true, and yet they rot.

AMOS.

The frame rots, not the courage or the faith ;
They live for ever in the thoughts of men.

ARVAH.

Until we rot ourselves, then they are lost.

AMOS.

Men's thoughts can never rot—they are eternal.
There is no fibre in the living thought,
That hath within itself seed of decay,
For ever we must think, and thinking be
Of that which we have thought.

ARVAH.

         I cannot follow you.
When I am dead my thought is dead.

AMOS.

          Not so.
When the poor frames that clog our thoughts are
   dead,
We think indeed.

ARVAH.

    The proofs—give me the proofs.

AMOS.

They are beyond my numbering—tradition,
Old records written down by sainted men,
Things passing Nature even now revealed
To such—the very fitness of all things—
As beasts have claws to grasp and teeth to tear,
So men have hearts to choose the good, and choosing,
Be happy evermore. All this my father
At leisure will expound. Dost thou not feel

That good and ill are placed before us now ;
That those who choose the ill oft seem to thrive,
And yet if we choose ill we choose the worse ;
And why, if man lives not beyond earth's space ?

ARVAH.

It is a wondrous thought, yet scarcely comes
Quite like a stranger to the mind—rather
As one expected though not known—a thought
That some I ween would welcome in the porch
Did they but know it true.

AMOS,

        And thou shalt know it.
Look out now on the plain—the sweet calm plain :
It hath a different reading.

ARVAH.

        Read it thou.

AMOS.

I see a beauty thrown upon the earth
Like image on a lake fragile as it,
And yet the rendering of that most real.
I see a sleep that mocks me not with calm,
But *is* calm—calm, that God so often gives
To nerve us for the struggles still to come.
I know death lurks beneath yon mist of light,

And fear and rapine crouch through all the trees;
But the fair moon is true, and the soft flowers:
And we can do our duty, rest, and hope.   ·

ARVAH.

Nay, it may be we cannot rest but basely.

AMOS.

Then are we of the chosen ones indeed:
The warrior spirits whom the Lord hath called
To be most noble on the earth.

ARVAH.

                Most noble.

I think I'd rather be most happy if
I could.

AMOS.

         It is the same; the noblest here
Are happiest in heaven.

ARVAH.

           And where is heaven?

AMOS.

In death, when we have died not to be base.

ARVAH.

I think I almost follow now.   Your God
Is the Great Maker of all things, and good—
Some thought like this floated before my childhood—

And heaven is the unbodied spirit's state
That did no wrong.

AMOS.

　　　　　　And thus can know its Maker,
And knowing Him must love.

ARVAH.

　　　　　　　　Must then all love
Who know ?

AMOS.

　　　　All who are pure.   Who sin have hate
Of Him engrafted in their being, such
That in the unnatural conflict in themselves
They find an agony eternal.

ARVAH.

　　　　　　That
I think I almost follow too.   To hate
And hate oneself for hating while we know
That God is good, and we are bad, must be
A pang unutterable.   Even now
To forfeit love that's ours by our own baseness
Were fire of soul might well scorch out our lives.

AMOS.

Which then compact of deathless essence all
Can but endure the unendurable *
For evermore.

　　　* A thought taken from a paper in the *Spectator*.

ARVAH.

Thus choosing painful good
Rather than pleasant baseness, we have gained
In truth, nobility at once and joy.

AMOS.

Even so.

ARVAH.

It is a glorious faith.   A faith
Firm-held might well make us despise their threats
Who'd frighten us from virtue.

AMOS.

And give strength
To war against ourselves—our baser selves—
When they'd betray us.

ARVAH.

Therefore are you good,
You and your father and your brother Seth.
How worship you your God?

AMOS.

With our whole lives.

ARVAH.

But have you not some special pomp of praise ?

AMOS.

We give the firstlings of our flocks and fruits.

H

ARVAH.

Give how ?

AMOS.

Upon the altar, holocausts.

ARVAH.

Not the poor gentle lambs that bleat—not them ?

AMOS.

Yes, even them.   Such is the law ; it may be
The beast feels not the pain it seems to feel.

ARVAH.

But wherefore harden thus our hearts with blood ?

AMOS.

I know not, but my father knows ; and they
May find the answer who, being pure, would die
To give God joy and man.   It well may be
That thou shalt find it, lady.

ARVAH.

                                        Nay, 'tis mine
To learn, not teach.

AMOS.

                              Would I were better teacher.
Perhaps were all things plain there were no merit
In serving God through simple selfishness.

ARVAH.

And since we feel, who yet but know we live,
'Twere better far to die than lose the good
Within ourselves that makes us love our life,
How much more when we hope to live again,
Though hope be not yet certainty.

AMOS.

                But hope
In God must trust in Him, for doubt were sin.

ARVAH.

In those who once *believe*; I have but *heard*
And heard of mystery without the answer.
If we may live again, our loves still live;
Is it not so?

AMOS.

          Most certainly, more pure
And strong.

ARVAH.

        Nay, that I doubt, but let it be;
And those we love shall know how we have loved
   them.

AMOS.

They shall be part of us—soul wrapped in soul.

ARVAH.

I must go in; I may be missed.   Lo, now,
I too can look out on yon pallid show

Of peace, and feel but sad, not hopeless ; sad,
For it is beautiful.

AMOS.

Most beautiful.
See how the snowy flakes of light fall coldly
Through all the resting leaves.   Bright, bright, O
  queen,
But chill as hope that hath not warmed to trust.

ARVAH.

Call me not queen ; I am a simple maid—
A very sad one.   Might not this tracery
Of shadowy boughs seem a great spider's clutch
Would drag to ruin ?   Bear with me—I'm foolish !
They say we're ever sad looking our last
On face we hate not.   I shall never see
Quite that same face again—never, never.

AMOS.

To-morrow night.

ARVAH.

Not so.   The moon shall then
Be older by a day.   Good night.

Act IV.

SCENE I.

The grove before Saleph's cottage.

SALEPH, ARVAH, and HEVIRAH.

SALEPH.

The Lord made Adam's body of the slime,
By slow gradations, from the primal cell
In order.   All things by Him are made in order;
The very breaches of our natural laws
But mark a higher order infinite.
Were He to frame a flower to glad that path,
And for that end alone, 'twould take its place
In the great sequence of botanic law,
And we might trace its germs, were we so wise,
To the first mystery of floral life;
But Eve He formed from Adam's rib, a sign
That he should cleave to her for evermore.
And still God's love hath been with constancy

Of man and wife from that day unto this ;
For Irad, son of Seth's son, loved his spouse
Naamah well while she was fair ; but when
A loathsome fever harrowed all her frame,
Seaming her smooth face into ruts, he prayed
The Lord that he might have another wife.
And when his prayer was heard, but so that he
Should put Naamah straightway from his tent,
And never see her more, he thanked the Lord.
Yet on the morn he set forth, when he turned,
And saw her standing by the door, and knew
She wept, he felt his heart grow heavy too,
And thought of all her love and gentle care,
And grieved much that she was stricken so.
And as he journeyed onward, heavier
Still grew his thoughts, and still he deemed it
    harder
That he might never see her face again ;
And though he looked on faces fair as hers,
They were not hers, and still he longed for hers.
Until one morning, as he rose, he thought
He would go back to her ; and when he saw
His tent, he saw her standing on the mound
Watching where she had watched him as he went.
And he was glad that he had come ; but she,
When she had seen he was alone, ran down
To meet him with a litle cry, and lo !

Her face was smooth as when he wooed her first,
For the good Lord was glad that he was constant.

ARVAH.

It is a pretty tale ; and yet, had I
Been she, I think I had not welcomed him.

HEVIRAH.

Nor I—not on the mound before the door ;
I would have looked cross first, to punish him.

ARVAH.

I think I never could have loved him more ;
It was so base to leave me in my sorrow.

SALEPH.

Alas ! my daughter, it were ill for us
If God were as implacable as thou.

ARVAH.

Yet when the angels fell, they fell for ever.

SALEPH.

As they *were* angels, we are only men ;
It is the weakness of our grosser selves
That makes His mercy part of justice.*

* Faber.

* H 4

Enter Amos.

AMOS.

                              Father,
'Tis time you rested from the heat of noon
And words.   I'll lead you to your couch within,
Craving the pardon of your pupils here.

ARVAH.

Most freely given.   Let me help you, sir ;
We two will con our questions over well,
To puzzle you when next we meet.

SALEPH.

                              That's well ;
The more you ask the more I shall be pleased.
Truth ever loves an honest questioner
But where is Seth ?   It was his wont to come.

AMOS.

I have not seen him since the morning meal.

SALEPH.

Please raise thine arm—I wonder why he came not?
                    [*Exeunt* SALEPH *and* AMOS.

ARVAH.

'Tis a sad tale—that tale of Paradise—

HEVIRAH.

Most sad.   If our great mother sinned not, Cain
And Abel had been loving friends.   Alas !
When those who are most near are most unkind
'Tis well to think it is the blood of Eve
That poisons all our veins, and to forgive
When they are sorry.   I have seen our father
Gaze after you ere now as we would gaze
After those angels of whom Saleph tells ;
If he but dared, he never would have wronged you.

ARVAH.

And therefore he had made me like a devil.
If he had had his will I was a devil.
I tell you, sister, the old man speaks nobly ;
If there be One that from the infinite heights
Above, a true paternity all holy,
Still leans o'er such as you and me—to Him
I turn—He is my only Father.

HEVIRAH.

                             Say

He is my Father—not my only one—
When Eve forgave her son the murderer,
Why cannot you forgive—he *is* your father.

ARVAH.

Cain killed the body.   Had my father held
His dagger to my throat as my sharp refuge,
I could have thanked him.   Even now I go
Back to that town to 'scape a blot more light
A hundredfold than was my father's planning.

HEVIRAH.

He is a son of Cain, so pity him.
When shall we go ?

ARVAH.

                I go alone, Hevirah.

HEVIRAH.

Alone !   Alone !   Surely I heard you wrongly.

ARVAH.

My child, if things are well, I'll come for you ;
If ill, your little arm could do no good,
And I were the less resolute.

HEVIRAH.

                        Alone !
It is not true—you never said ' Alone '—
You cannot go alone, for I will follow.
Did we not say that we should die together ?

ARVAH.

Thou art so young—'twere pity thou shouldst die,
My gentle one—I could not see thee dead.
I were all hate of man, and more than man,
If thou wert dead.

HEVIRAH.

O, Arvah, speak not so ;
I shall not die—you shall not die, indeed—
Let me be by your side on earth, and I
Shall be there evermore.

ARVAH.

And the red blood
The red red blood, will dabble all this breast,
The little breast I kissed ere you might stand.
I could not bear it.

HEVIRAH.

It will turn to rubies,
Pink-tinging rubies, in the smile of God,
Which you can kiss and kiss eternally.

ARVAH.

O sweet, my sister, stay ; I will come back.

HEVIRAH.

We shall come back if all goes well. I love
The kind old man and Amos—aye, and Seth.

ARVAH.

He speaks as you—the younger one—says death
Is not a sleep but an awakening
When we know more than now.

HEVIRAH.

Such is their faith—
My faith—our faith—there we will go together.
Oh Arvah, my own sister, I will thank you,
As never yet was sister thanked by sister.
'Twere death indeed were we to separate.
When shall we go ?—to-morrow let us go ;
The idiot by the gate will starve without us ;
To-morrow, yes, to-morrow.

ARVAH.

It may be
Our friends here will along with us, Hevirah.

HEVIRAH.

Amos and Seth ?

ARVAH.

E'en they—they have strong arms

HEVIRAH.

And hearts—they love you dearly—Amos does,
At least, and Seth, I think he loves you too ;

ARVAH.

Why do you doubt it ? Know you where he's gone ?

HEVIRAH.

Not I.

ARVAH.

He tracked a tiger yesterday,
And says he'll bring the skin to me ere night.

HEVIRAH.

And wherefore?   It would not have done you harm,
Not like the panther slain hard by our sleep:
I think I know who killed that panther, Arvah.

ARVAH.

You little wise wise wench!

HEVIRAH.

                    Yet never spoke of it.
Which do you like the best?

ARVAH.

                    Why must I tell you?

HEVIRAH.

Because I am your conscience—so you said;
And conscience must know everything, of course.

ARVAH.

But it finds out—we do not speak to conscience,
Nor you nor I—and no one else has any.

HEVIRAH.

Nay, we consult it.

ARVAH.

Do we? Well—Seth's bigger,
And has a laugh I like—I'd rather laugh
With Seth.   And then he has an arm might reach
Strong Zoar himself over his guard—I think
I'd rather fight with him than with his brother;
I mean upon his side.

HEVIRAH.

And yet a head
May often more advantage than an arm.

ARVAH.

I'd rather speak with Amos—he can feel
What one has felt when we scarce know we felt it,
Can knit our puzzled words into plain speech,
And sometimes finds the answer that we long for—
I'd rather speak with Amos.

HEVIRAH.

'Tis not thus
I would be answered.

ARVAH.

How then, little one?

HEVIRAH.

I asked which do you love the best?

ARVAH.

O love!

Love is a big word, conscience—I love you.

HEVIRAH.

And I shall love him best who so loves Arvah.
But which does Arvah love?

ARVAH.

I love them both;

One since he stemmed a hundred in our streets,
And from afar I watched him towering still
By head and shoulders o'er the baffled crowd,
And I would save him from his deed.

HEVIRAH.

Sending

The chain he flaunts so now.

ARVAH.

Ah, there it is:

Since conscience will know all, and thou art she,
I must confess to feel I harm him, conscience.
When first we met, through all the many threads,
Some vain, some generous, springing straight to act

Or word, there was entwined a love of Him
They serve and of his father—aye, and brother—
That gave a golden glimmer to the rest.
Now he but thinks of me and of himself—
Most common thoughts.

HEVIRAH.
And Amos, what of him?

ARVAH.

Oh, he is different.

HEVIRAH.
How different?

ARVAH.

He's not as tall as Seth.

HEVIRAH.
No, nor as ruddy;
And, sister, he grows paler day by day,
Why should that be?

ARVAH.
Belike he, as the youngest,
Was used to choice at feasts, and so now starves
Since you and I eat all the good things up.

HEVIRAH.
You heartless one! You know the feast he craves
Are sister Arvah's words.

Hush! here he comes.
I vow the red has left his cheek for yours.

Enter AMOS.

AMOS.

My father found your gathered flowers, Hevirah,
And begs you go to him that he may thank you.

[*Exit* HEVIRAH.

The old man loves the flowers and the child.

ARVAH.

A taste in age most beautiful.   Long years
Lose half their winter loving youth and flowers.

AMOS.

Age makes not winter in the human heart ;
Its frosts are selfishness and sordid thoughts,
My father's is as tender as the child's,
Therefore he loves her young companionship.

ARVAH.

And she loves him ; 'tis sad that they must part.

AMOS.

Part! part! and wherefore should they part ?

ARVAH.

To-morrow
I must return, and she returns with me.

I

AMOS.

To-morrow!   And you say it thus unmoved—
I heard her laugh as I came through the trees-
To-morrow!

ARVAH.

        Yes, she laughs; why should she not ?
Why should we not ?   All joys must have an end ;
Then always laugh ; it is the wiser plan.

AMOS.

It is a noble plan when pain is felt,
But cruelty when we ourselves give pain.

ARVAH.

I have no faith in pain except my own,
So even on your showing must still laugh.

AMOS.

You cannot think your words ; it were too monstrous.

ARVAH.

I'll think, sir, what I choose.   If I'm a monster,
Why, I will laugh at that.

AMOS.

        And you *can* laugh.
We were so happy in our peaceful lives,
Knowing no other pleasure ere you came.

ARVAH.

And now will have your peace quite back again
When we are gone.

AMOS.

       Your presence, like the glow
Of summer sun, too bright, has withered all.
There's not a spot where you once walked or spoke
But will be consecrate by separate pang
To memory.   My father—my dear father—
My failing father—

ARVAH.

       Peace ! Are you a man
With grace and mercy in you, as I deemed,
And keenest mastery of others' thoughts ?
It cannot be, or you would spare me now,
Nor make my cup too bitter to be drank.
Think you I go to lay me down on roses ?
I tell you, man, I have a task to do
Might tax your powers and stronger powers than
    yours.
Speak not to me of aches or pains or pangs.
I and my sister face these things in truth,
Not in mere painting of well-pointed words.

AMOS.

And think you, Arvah, that I did not know it ?
Think you one chance of all your desperate lot

Hath been unweighed by me ?   My nightly visions
Could tell a different tale, and sleep refused
In dread of dream too near reality.
I spoke as I have spoken but to move
Your purpose with the thought of others' sorrow,
As the last chance.

ARVAH.

Your hand ; pray pardon me.
It were a pain, a keen one through them all,
To think you were not what I deemed—oh ! friend
Now I can face my lot with braver heart.

AMOS.

Nay, face it not ; be ruled, and stay with us.

ARVAH.

And give the lie to my whole life ; be false
To those that I have made : nay more, be false
To Him whose love you teach me is man's heaven.
If such there be, I am His messenger,
If such there be—nay, in this hour I feel
That such there *is*, and know Him in His message.

AMOS.

O be more merciful ; it cannot be
God's will that you should give this pain—my father—
Speak to my father, and be ruled by him.

ARVAH.

Why should I speak to him? Were he to counsel
My stay, I were unmoved; if otherwise,
'Twere pain to him.

AMOS.

Will nothing move you?

ARVAH.

Nothing.

AMOS.

O God be merciful to her and me!
Arvah, I love you—love the ground you tread on!
Would give my life to save your finger's ache.
O Arvah! my bright queen! my beautiful!
Stay here and I will go, I and my brother.
You two can guard our father in his age.

ARVAH.

I thank you, Amos—let us go together!
I think I should not fear were you with me.

AMOS.

Give me your hand—one kiss upon your hand;
'Twill seal our contract for this earth and heaven.

ARVAH.

Not now, not now—the time may come—not now.
O friend, I'm your's; but kiss me not—not yet.

I am the virgin warrior of the Lord;
It seemed that as you spake I knew His will.
No kiss must rest upon that hand until
Its task is done.

            Hark! some one comes—your brother—
I cannot meet him now.   He hath not seen me.
An hour hence I'll be here again.   But heed not
My foolish words; you still must care your father;
It were a double death were you with me.
I must away—an hour—one hour.   [*Exit* ARVAH.

AMOS.

                   My queen!
My bright queen!—Arvah!   O, my God, she must
Not go!—'tis not Thy will—not Thine.

Enter SETH.

SETH.

Amos! what do you here?

AMOS.

              But now she left me—
Our guest—we spoke together.

SETH.

                 Where is she?

AMOS.

I know not.

SETH.

Know not!   And your icy tone
Gives sharper edge to icy words! B y heaven
I like them not ; there's much I like not, Amos.
I have been thinking as I walked, thinking—
I am no child to let your cunning fool me.

AMOS.

Why speak you thus to me ?—when have I wronged
  you ?

SETH.

Well, well, take care! A word in time, you know—
I like not too much these vain chatterings—
My father were best teacher, as I think.

AMOS.

Perhaps I heard not truly ; otherwise
There seems a something in your tone fits not
The time, or you, or me.

SETH.

Fits not! fits not!
Are you my judge, pray?   But a truce to this.
I have been thinking all day, as I said,
And now will speak.   I am your elder brother.
Come not between that girl and me, or else
As sure as there is Heaven above us both,
If you will cross my path !—well, look you to it !

[*Exit.* SETH.

*I 4

AMOS.

Are we to have another Cain?   And yet
Why should she be so wronged? He must have seen
I loved her first when he had naught to throw
To daughter of her race but words for dogs.
And now that she is pleased with my deep love,
Must I forsake her at his wanton beck?
Hath she not pains enough that he must give
This last and crowning one? She will but scorn him;
But scorn be pain, for she hath loved him well.
Scorn him?—our Seth—it seems but yesterday
I sat beside his bed after the fever.
And he—well, well, it matters not—O Seth,
Seth, Seth, if I but thought you loved her first
I would have kept my heart whole, or have let
It burst ere it had angered you! But now,
Why should she be so wronged?—Arvah, our guest.
It was no sudden thought that threat of his,
But must have come, though my poor words pro-
    voked it
Then, knowing that she wished not for his presence.
How beautiful she looked—and soft, so soft—
With all the woman in her drooping eye
As she withdrew her hand. How it can change,
That eye of hers. I love it better still
In each and every mood except its pain,

And yet most love it then.   My friend, my queen,
O God, look down on her and give her peace ;
All things are possible to Thee.   Thy fires
May fall upon the sinful town ; Thy plague
Stretch the grey tyrants rotting in its streets ;
Thy will can pluck from Seth's heart this quick love
That may but scorch, not warm. All things are Thine ;
And what seems mine take Thou for her dear sake.
To make her happy what were life to me ;
Sooner or later she would know the gift,
And knowing love me as I now love her.
I do remember when we stood that night,
Watching the plain, she fancied the bent arms
Of shadowy boughs that circled all our feet,
Was some weird ruin's lean and spidery clutch
That lay in wait to drag us to its breast.
Was it a flash of more than mortal light
That warned her brave soul thus against my love ?
Forbid it, Heaven ! Then I had scorned the thought ;
I was a man, and I was by her side.
Well, I will scorn it still ; I am a man still--
A man ! but am I man enough to bear
Unmoved rough words and fierce, perchance a blow?
And even if so brave, may not my patience
Provoke him but the more ; still resolute
In act, as I must still be resolute ?
O God ! shall brother's blood be on my soul ?

Not shed by me ; not shed, but given ; forbid it
Most Merciful ! And thou great martyred Saint's
Pure Spirit who art with me in this hour,
Let not thy blood, once shed, plead now in vain !
My altar stands as thine ; still it must stand.
But though my life should be the offering,
Let it fall cleanly nor pollute my brother ;
Let it be pledge of joy to her I love,
Not a new ruin !

SCENE II.

The interior of Saleph's cottage.

SALEPH and HEVIRAH.

SALEPH.   (*Reading*).

' And lo ! the woman shall redeem the woman,
And in the late days men shall see her praise,
Like dew at morning gladden all the earth.
Then shall the name of mother be most blessed
Of all names except One, and its sweet sheen
Adown the memory of childish years
Be oft the pure vision of tired wretches
That drag their sinful lives out in the noon,
Till when the great account is closed at last,
And closing is unfolded to the world,

All men shall see that scarce one soul was saved
Except through woman.'
(*He shuts the scroll*).
Such the prophecy ;
How dost thou like it, child ?

HEVIRAH.
Oh, father Saleph !
How I would try to save a soul !   And think you
As many women shall be saved as men ?

SALEPH.
Nay more—or so I'd gather from that prophecy,
For charity begins at home.

HEVIRAH.
And in heaven
We shall be men and women just as here ?

SALEPH.
Most certainly, even as the Cherubim
And Seraphim have each their separate gifts
Wherewith they honour God eternally,
So in the full completion of our state
Two human choirs shall blend in perfect praise.

HEVIRAH.
What can our souls be like without our bodies ?

SALEPH.

Why, like our thoughts, for such in truth they are.
If thou shouldst lose thy hand thou losest not thought,
No offshoot of the soul, but just a hand ;
And so with legs, and arms, and all the rest.

HEVIRAH.

But if I lose my head I cannot think ?

SALEPH.

Rather your head will think while life is there.
Brain is the seat of thought as eye of sight,
And yet the thought and sight are not of flesh,
But of the soul imprisoned in the flesh ;
Just as from this dark chamber we can see
But through the door, yet not the door thus sees,
But we within.

HEVIRAH.

I think I follow you.
Yet what can thought be without shape ? I cannot
Fancy myself all thought—and if our frames
Are prisons, why retake them in the end ?

SALEPH.

We scarce can fancy what we have not felt
Until the appointed time for feeling comes,
And when we blest regain our bodies blest,

We shall find enchanted palaces not prisons,
Like such unfettered by now laws of matter.
Nothing in man God-given is ever lost,
Rather his choicest gifts are here but germs
Of destined growth beyond mere mortal fancy;
So in the full completion of all things
We shall retake these frames that seemed to rot,
Yet souls shall nothing lose, but we all gain,
Thus perfected at last.

HEVIRAH.

What shall our joy be
For ever and for ever?

SALEPH.

Knowing and loving.

HEVIRAH.

Yet we shall know of pain unutterable.
There is a tale they tell of their god Moloch,
Of whose dear gift they feign sweet sounds to be,
When a vain fool would strive with him in song,
The conquering god had the wretch flayed all quick,
Smiling himself, as he lay on the grass,
A cruel smile, whose thought still makes me shudder,
But more with hate than fear.

SALEPH.

An honest hate.

HEVIRAH.

And yet the shepherd's pain were joy to that
Which we shall see in hell eternally.

SALEPH.

My child, if thou wouldst stand on yonder plain
This sultry noon and gaze upon the sun,
Thou might'st not trace its disk, yet it were there,
All perfect as at evening in the west.
So with the justice of our Lord and God;
He hath no loose capriciousness in pain,
But ever acts by His eternal laws,
As perfect as Himself—being Himself—
The punishment of sin is of the sin,
Not of the Lord.   Wert thou in sudden rage
To strike and slay a gentle courteous child,
That loved thee and ne'er wronged, the deed were
    thine,
And all its load of never-dying pain.
She would not punish thee, but thy own wrong
Would scourge thee evermore.   So when we sin
We injure goodness infinite, and thus,
When time and all its littleness is past,
Are infinite in pain.

HEVIRAH.

        Then siu is pain,
For evermore and of itself the pain,
Ill, too, beyond all chance of remedy.

SALEPH.

When chosen in full light with steadfast gaze
Of its own nature, yes.

HEVIRAH.

Yet God can pardon.

SALEPH.

He can, but how? My child, these are great thoughts,
Perchance ill-seeming thy green years,
And yet I am impelled to speak to thee
As you sit there, young girl, beside my couch,
As I ne'er spoke to my own sons. It may be
In the stern order of eternal justice
That none may pardon—not the Lord Himself—
In justice to Himself who is His justice—
Unless fit penalty be paid for sin.

HEVIRAH.

Then sinners have no hope, for none can pay.

SALEPH.

None save the Lord, who still is infinite
In payment given as in the debt He makes.

HEVIRAH.

O father, is thy thought that God can pardon,
Yet pardoning must suffer for the sin?

SALEPH.

I said these things surpassed thy tender years,
And mortal minds which may not sound them quite,
For though God still must act in all most well,
He acts not from necessity but choice;
Yet thank the Lord, my child, Who loves thee dearly.

HEVIRAH.

And could the great God suffer aught for us,
The dust-specks on His universe?

SALEPH.

My little one,
As God is justice, mercy, beauty, order,
So is He too self-sacrifice and love,
And love is wonderful in all its ways.

HEVIRAH.

Now do I shudder not at hell but sin—
And yet the body burns too—what can burn it?

SALEPH.

The soul that blest can make the body blest,
And damned make hell of that which was its flesh.

HEVIRAH.

Which God gave for its joy.   O, father Saleph!
Why do not all men know these things, and so
Be good?

SALEPH.

My child, the time will come when all
Shall know them, yet the world be scarcely better.
Many will turn the very gift to sin,
Sinning the more that God is merciful.

HEVIRAH.

And will none long to give their inmost hearts,
Their very heart of hearts, in hymn of praise,
If such may be of solace to His love,
Poor love, that thus is spilt out on the earth?
Alas! I am a child, and see these things
All dimly through the mist, as we just catch
The great trees looming on an autumn morn
Ere yet the freshness of the glorious world.
But, father Saleph, God is stern at times:
Witness His heavy hand on Cain and Eve.

SALEPH.

As is the mother's who would chide her flock
From fire that burns yet flickers pleasantly.
It well may be we had no fear of sin
But for the temporal ruin God hath sent
To warn us weaklings from the eternal pest.
Surely I hear a step!

K

Enter SETH.

SETH.

Not here—Hevirah,

Where is your sister?

HEVIRAH

When I saw her last

She spoke with Amos in the grove.

SETH.

With Amos!

I come from him.

SALEPH.

My son, where hast thou been?

We missed you much all day.

SETH

Missed me!   By heaven,

There were who missed me little, as I think.

I have been fool'd, father, by lying trail.

SALEPH.

More like the trail lied not, but thy impatience

Marred too short toil—always thy fault, my son,

As this scroll minds me, which with all its fellows

Were treasure-chambers ever locked to thee,

But that my constancy o'erbare thy rashness.

SETH.

Old musty treasures!

SALEPH.

      Musty! Son, blaspheme not
The blessed gift of God to darkened man,
Short-lived and darkened. But for that great gift
The little light which each one wins were lost
With him, and never hoard descend
Of common knowledge to the sons of men,
For thoughts held but in words vary as they.

SETH.

And could not God teach me as He taught him
Who wrote that scroll?

SALEPH.

      Doubtless He could, but will not.
To him He gave the thoughts, to me the art
Thus to decipher them and to transmit it
To thee in thy good patience. We may not
Choose ways for Him who gives, but He for us.

SETH.

Let those who will grow pale o'er crabbed symbols;
Give me the sunshine and the glorious play
Of young blood through strong limbs uncramped by
   such things.

A spade a spade I know, and sword a sword,
And they are at my hand.   As for the rest,
The mystic dreams that hang 'twixt earth and heaven,
Here is a child whose years six hands may count,
Yet seems as skilled already in such lore
As many who've been puzzling all their lives.
And so you know not where your sister is ?
Well, well, I'll leave you to your lesssons.

[Exit SETH.

SALEPH.

Follow him.

There is a restless spirit in his eye
I like not.   Follow him—yes, follow him,
And, when thou mayest, coax his steps hitherward,
Hevirah.

SCENE III.

The same part of the grove as before.

Enter ARVAH.

ARVAH.

It is the second hour, and yet he comes not.
Fair trees, dear trees, where first I—Oh Amos,
Why come you not ?   The time is very short,
So short, and I have much to say.   And yet
When he does come I think I shall not speak,

But listen, listen, ever listen. I—
Can this be I? I do not know myself.
It was not I that kissed the footstepped clay
In the old winter fields where he hath worked.
I took away my hand, but I kissed that—
There was no sin in that—but was it I—
I—Arvah, archer, that hath laughed ere now?
And yet why should I shame me of my love?
All woman for one hour, if but for one,
To thank the man who gives his all to me.
O Amos, Amos, come! the time's so short.
To-morrow I must go, to-morrow, to-morrow,
And yet the world has grown so bright. O love,
The fields where thou shalt toil seemed heaven to
  me;
Scarce could I turn me from them but the hour
Had passed, or so I hoped, and still you come not.
To night we'll wander forth once more as when
We stood together fronting the pale moon,
And with the words there seemed to come an echo
Of an eternal gladness from the hills,
Waking up yearnings deeper far than they
In this lone heart of mine. My love, my love,
Thou wert the angel of the Lord thy God,
That He hath sent to me in my sore need.
'Tis little thing to part this mortal frame
When we both still can think and love. And yet

But yesterday as I stood by the stream
My golden circlet glimmered on the wave,
And as I looked I knew that I was fair,
And thought of thee the while.   I would not choose
To lose aught that thou lovest in poor me.
In heaven all shall be fair as I, and thou
No gainer in thy love that she is fair.
What now ?

Enter SETH *hurriedly,* HEVIRAH *following.*

SETH.

My brother—Amos—have you seen him ?
There is a camel's track quite fresh seeking
The East, and his hath joined it.

ARVAH.

Why so pale ?
What mean those scared looks ?   Speak ! in God's
    name, speak !

SETH.

Gone, gone !   O Lady, who would give his life
To save a sin and for another's joy,
May enter Paradise, but entering there
Must die.

ARVAH.

I've heard so, or I think I have,
I've heard so many things these days. Speak, speak !
What horrible thought can thus unman you? Speak !

SETH.

Amos tries now the venture.

ARVAH.

Amos! Amos!

SETH.

I never saw a camel's track before
Upon this plain—it is the hand of God.
He hath been chosen. The Lord hath thrown me off.
An hour ago we parted with hot words.

ARVAH.

You! you! Hot words to Amos—to your brother,
The brother that so loved you. Why what madness
Possessed you?

SETH.

Ask me not that.

ARVAH.

Ask you not?
Speak! speak! Why were those words?

SETH.

I cannot answer.

ARVAH.

Cannot? By Cain I'll wrench the answer from you
As I would wrench the jaws of hound that tore me.
What were your words?

SETH.

They were of you.

ARVAH.

Of me!

SETH.

I wished to make you wife, and told him so.

ARVAH.

Me wife! Me? me?—me wife! and threatened him?
Tell me but that you threatened him. I see it
In guilty eye that dare not look at me,
Nor ever at an honest thing again.
Your God has thrown you off. Just God,
He were not mine had He not thrown you off,
You vile degenerate beast! Why, look you now,
There's not a greybeard in the streets of Cain
But in my eyes will tower above you far
As towers the eagle o'er the carrion thing
That rots upon the ground. They know no good;
You, father that is mirror of his God,
A brother like—O man, I cannot speak,
My loathing eats my heart, but is too big
For words. Out of my way; out, out! Sight of you
Is as a mildew.   [*Exit* ARVAH.

SETH.

All, all! all is lost.
For her I gave my God and she—and yet not so,
'Twas but myself I sought—myself in all,

And found my marring, as is just, most just.
' A vile, degenerate beast ! '   I heard, nor answered.
I could not answer it, for it was true.
Yet has the time been when I felt, I, Seth,
Compeer of angels who but love their Maker
With their whole hearts as I, and may not suffer
As I, nor dare as I'd dare for the Lord.
I never loved her ; never thought of woman
With longing dream as Amos.   Therefore it was
My father sent me to those streets of Cain.
Strange how I grow so wise thus of a sudden.
And now my master sin hath ruined all—
The sin I knew not of, or thought a virtue.
I could not see another win the prize,
Not for the prize, but that it should be won,
And not by me.   Therefore am I accursed,
Thrown off by God and man.   I dare not face
My father—dare face none—here will I lie.
Beast, grovel on the earth !

> [*Throws himself on the ground.*

HEVIRAH
                    Seth, brother Seth !

SETH.
Who calls ?   You here, Hevirah !

HEVIRAH.
                    I have followed
Your steps, yet dared not speak.

SETH.

Dared not !   By Heaven, then,
You feared a hound too whipped to tear a mouse.

HEVIRAH.

Yet had a tiger evil times of it, I ween,
Within his reach.   Words are but words ; thin air,
That vibrates and is still.

SETH.

                    As life is air,
Or something as impalpable.   I tell you
One keen word might outweigh a hundred lives ;
Yet not for words I grieve, but thoughts, and they
Are of the essence of us all.   Give me
Pure thoughts, and take the rest.   I had them once.

HEVIRAH.

And shall have them again.   Am I too bold ?
You are not angel yet, but just a man,
And God hath proved it to you.

SETH.

                    Man !—no, beast.
That was her word.

HEVIRAH.

Tut, heed it not.   We girls
Weigh not our accents as a moneyer
His coinèd bits of gold.

SETH.

She may not weigh
Her words; I weigh my deeds.

HEVIRAH.

And find them wanting.
Are you not child of Adam, who hath sin
Engrainèd in his being?

SETH.

One week since
I felt no stain within me.   The light specks
That lay upon the surface were scarce mine,
But his who sinned the first.   Now I have sinned
Deeper than he.

HEVIRAH.

And shall like him repent,
And be more loved than you were loved before.
Knowing your weakness and your need of love.
Perchance that thought of sinlessness was pride
Which deadly rust had eaten all your lustre,
But that the very roughness of your fall
Thus saves you.

SETH.

But an hour ago I laughed
At thee and at thy wisdom.

HEVIRAH.

So laugh still.
Think this the simple prattle of a child
Who loves thee very dearly, brother Seth.

SETH.

Laugh? laugh?   I think I shall ne'er laugh again,
And yet thy loving words make me a man.
My brother's track is fresh upon the sands ;
It may be that my arm can serve him still.
I'll follow.

HEVIRAH.

And kind angels with thee.

Act Ⅴ.

SCENE I.

The grove before Saleph's cottage.

SALEPH and HEVIRAH.

SALEPH.

                        Thy sister watches
Still on the furthest rise?

HEVIRAH.

                        Since morning, father,
And so will watch till night.

SALEPH.

                        One will return;
And yet, on such a quest, if both were taken,
Were it not gain?

HEVIRAH.

                        Upon the desert plain
There is no track.

SALEPH.

> None—it is ever pathless

As a great ocean.

HEVIRAH.

> Yet in Paradise

Are rivers—or a river—whither flows it?

SALEPH.

I know not—it may dip into the earth.

HEVIRAH.

Our river leaps from misty cavern depths,
And tales, old as itself with shadowy vagueness,
Hint at no common source.

SALEPH.

> Who may essay

To trace the working of the Lord our God,
Through all the mighty depths o'er which we stand?
There may be suns beneath our feet as great
As that above, worlds within worlds for ever.
It well may be the stream thou tellest of
Flows through deep caverned ways from Paradise.
O child, perchance my sons die now of thirst,
While almost leaning on swift waves beneath them.

HEVIRAH.

If they return not ere to-night, my sister
Herself attempts to follow.

SALEPH.

It were madness.
Thou must dissuade her from it—tracks are lost
Upon the sands as motion through a stream.

HEVIRAH.

Then how could Seth hope to o'ertake his brother?

SALEPH.

His path was penance, and as such was held.

HEVIRAH.

He scarce can grieve more than my sister grieves,
Who brought the seeds of discord to your peace.

SALEPH.

Let her not grieve.   She is heaven's instrument!
Ere yet you came I knew one son was called;
E'en now I know that one of them returns,
It may be both.   Strange are the ways of God.
This quest may be but trial-strengthening
For greater things to come.   Perchance the sin,
The fearful sin, that stains thy guilty tribe,
May from the lightened earth be swept for ever.
I would not keep one soul back from the Lord,
And from the appointed paths that He hath laid
Through momentary pang and severance.
Blood freely given is the great purge of sin,

Witness lambs slain in solemn sacrifice;
The symbols of a symbol, and yet more,
Yet more than symbol is the blood of man.
Alas! what are earth's joys but as the glamour
Upon the waste the traveller tells of, where sands
Will gleam a lake before the failing wretch,
Who sinks at last on the dry brink to die.
My boys! my boys! Oh pray for them, my child,
In this their fiery trial and the thirst.
They were so good to me, loving and good;
It seems but yesterday that little Seth
Sat where thou sittest now, when first my home
Made desolate, seemed waste for evermore,
A little smooth-cheeked thing not half thy height,
And as my eye lit on his face watching me
I felt that earth ——

HEVIRAH.

Hark! Lo where Arvah speeds,
Swift as an unloosed hound along the path.
O father, she has seen them.

ARVAH.

They come! Both come!

SCENE II.

The interior of the cottage.

SALEPH, SETH, AMOS, ARVAH and HEVIRAH.

SETH.

Methought, as I lay resting, a far wail
Broke on my startled ear, and swelled and swelled,
Till all my being sickened with its pain,
The pain of hideous shrieks of many men,
That had a ghastly cadence in their mingling,
As though some demon mocked the gift of song.
And lo, from the wide darkness dimly rose
What might be banners waving gloomily
O'er serried ranks that marched with measured tread,
Far as the eye could reach, through the pale night;
In dreadful muster black and shadowy
They grew upon me till I marked their faces,
Their horrible dead faces and stone eyes,
All set in rigour of keen agony.
The first were armèd as the sons of Cain,
With sword and bow, tall spear and shield pale-
　. glaring;
But still on each there gaped a death-wound wide.

And black blood hung in clots, and so they passed.
Then followed weaker forms, yet armed the same,
With the same horror in their dreadful eyes,
So terrible in pain I could not scorn them,
And yet methinks were they in live array
Alone I had not turned me from a hundred.
There was but one larger than we are now,
And in the centre of his pallid brow
Was a black wound as though a sling had bored it.
And they, too, passed; and then, with steadier tread,
Came men as small but with a noble bearing,
Even in death, and perfect limb, and armour
That shed a dismal lustre on the plain.
Some were in chariots, and their horses' eyes
Shone like keen stars, and one of firmest mould
Had dragging from the slow wheels of his car
The naked body of a man.   And lo!
E'en as they passed I thought the moon looked down,
Or some pale light like hers, upon the face
Supine upon the sand, and as a glory
It fell on the calm brow that smiled in death;
And grasping at my sword I would have sprang up
To right the fallen champion, but I might not,
Held down by sleep, or some strange power like sleep.
And still the phantoms passed in columns wider,
All ghastly as before.   And now I marked
The ensigns bore a sculptured eagle's form,

And bow and spear were gone and short straight
  sword,
And conqueror's mien retained even in doom
Told of a race that loved to close with foes.
And still they passed, and passed, and passed, tall
  men,
All clad in bronze from head to foot, on steeds
Bronze-clad as they; and then were strangest arms,
Or what seemed arms, like nothing I have seen.
But still the columns deepened, and the sounds
Of that dread music grew upon mine ear
Until I saw at every column's head
Grim ghostly bands that moaned their march of
  death;
And scarcely human were some forms that passed,
So burst and rent were they with gaping wounds.
And over all the plain I saw not sand,
But ruined cottages and blackened walls,
And children screaming as they starved, and towns
All charred and smouldering to their ruin, or
The ghosts of such, for all were dead I thought—
I knew that all were dead.   And then before me
Was a great ghastly city pale with fire,
A strange unearthly fire that made all shadowy.
I saw the very faces on the walls,
Dead faces glaring still o'er armèd men.
And even as once more I sought to rise,

Went up to heaven a universal shriek,
And I awoke, yet heard, as in mine ear,
'Such is thy crime in man.'

SALEPH.

Alas! my son,
It was no dream, but faithful vision given
Of that to come.

SETH.

Thus far I'd lined my path
By choosing guidance from a star, ere yet
The track or twilight faded utterly;
And now as I arose the sun just showed
Above the waste, and by that sign I went
Still facing eastward till the noontide rays
Smote on my tortured brow like rain of fire,
And toil and hunger and the burning thirst,
Had forced me from my purpose, but the dream
Upheld me ever, and the Hand of God
Thus seeming with me still although to chide.
And so I staggered on, praying in gasps,
And almost wildered with the light and blaze,
Till inch by inch the slow day sank, and once
Again I sought to guide me through the night.
But soon my eyes no more might fix the stars,
And strange weak dreams perplexed me, till I scarce
Could make it real where I was.   I think

I tried to call—the desert was so still—
And shouted ' Amos !' Shuddering at my voice,
I do remember now, so weak and hoarse,
When, lo ! a light, a light that was no star,
From out the furthest shadow glimmering shone,
And with it came the hope to drink, fierce hope
That made me strong enough to drag my limbs
Onward until I sank down senseless. Light
Was on my eyes when I awoke; a cup
Moistened my burning lips, and a pale face,
A woman's face, was leaning over me,
While at my side a little tiny child
Gazed at its great new toy. Above were palms
Half lit up by the lamp, and yet I saw
The stars shine through, then fainted once again.
But soon the freshening drink gave me new life,
And I could stand and walk, following the light
And her who bore it to a little hut
Mid leafy shrubs, and laid me down on moss;
Then eat of sun-dried fruits and drank cool milk,
And slept again, yet not before I knew
Her face that I had saved—her and her babe
In the white streets of Cain. Ere morn I dreamed
Another dream. Methought our Amos lay
All pale upon the ground, wounded and pale,
But with a light on him like his they dragged
Upon the sand behind the chariot wheels,

It may be there are those who see it now,
Yet was there pain and sadness in that look,
And as I saw I longed to get to him,
To tell him how I grieved, and ask his pardon;
But something held me and I could not stir.
And so I woke and saw the day had risen,
And ate again and felt my strength renewed,
And though the woman sought to keep me with her
Yet one day more, telling too how she strayed
Here from the north and with her child found roots,
And pleasant shade, and milk of many goats,
My dream was still before me and I went.
For now my longing grew with thought that Amos
Perchance was weak or lorn and wanted me.
Remembering all his care in olden time,
When from the fever I had scarce arisen;
Yea, thinking, too, my help might be the sign
God had forgiven me.   And so I went.
And for another morn toiled o'er the sand
Much dreaming of his love, and higher love
Than his, that I had hurt—fool that I was—
When lo! I saw a speck upon the plain
Uprising from the east, and it was he!

SALEPH.

My son, thou hast done well, and by my voice,
Thy earthly father's whom thou still hast honoured,

God bids thee henceforth be of peaceful mind,
For thou art pardoned.   Are we not all His own,
Waiting His high behests, which, stern it may be
Though loving, if my heart deceive me not,
Our Amos brings to us from Paradise ?

AMOS.

Stern are they, yet not stern ; to me not stern
Who have but seen to tell, yet scarce may tell
As I have seen, what is for all, not me,
So must essay.   When first I marked the track,
Fresh track hard by me as I stood in dream,
I doubted if the thought that filled my mind
Were fancy fooling or the call of God.
So oft had Seth spoken of Paradise,
And of the camel needed for the quest,
I scarce could help but think of it, when thus
The trail lay at my feet.   And when I reached
The beast standing amid the trees caparisoned,
I thought that I would mount and do its will,
Perchance to find in it the will of heaven,
Which oft may choose dumb instruments to guide
    us,
When all at variance is the unsettled mind,
Constant in wish to serve but dark to means.
And even as I sate me on its back
The beast threw up its head and eastward went.

Now well I knew that from the east it came not,
The springless desert where no man can live
And therefore chose the venture to the end.
Long ere the night had fallen we reached the sands,
But still sped on unswerving when it fell.
I doubt that camel ere so sped before.
The very motion made a breeze that fanned me,
Till as the sands flew past I almost fancied
The eastern stars grew nearer to my gaze.
At last, as I half thought to see the dawn,
A distant light bounded the furthest plain,
But was not like the dawn ; and as we neared
Its glow as of dimmed lustres from above
Illumed steep walls of sternest rock before me,
And mighty clouds that rolled out on their summits.
Then thought I of thy ride of old, my father,
And   wondered   would   mine   end   as   thine,   and
     longed—
But let that pass—for even then the camel
Gave a great cry as though it hailed afar
Its travels' bourne, and soon the tingèd light
Fell on its head and me and on the sand,
And fall of many waters smote my ear,
Till sands were gone, and in their place great rocks
Towered all around me, and the beast was standing
Beside a mighty stream that foamed and curled,

While almost overhead were the smooth cliffs
With a deep rent in them where swift waves
   broke;
And then my camel drank and I too drank,
And stupor came upon me, and I slept.

Have we not waked ere now on summer morns,
With a vague sense of gladness over all things,
As though to breathe were joy, and light were joy
Most keen—some faint far thought such waking
   gives
Of that which filled each fibre of my frame,
With blessedness beyond all natural fancy,
When through the half-closed portals of my sight
There came a sudden glory as of noontide;
Ere yet I knew it was no sun that beamed on me,
And on the reverend man beside me standing,
And on the strange-leafed beauty of a scene
That once beheld might grieve for evermore.
Yet was it most like sunshine at its brightest
That dazzled not nor scorched; and even then
I thought me of thy sunset song, Hevirah,
And the far west all gold; yet this not golden,
But rather, as light's essence, colourless,
Thus bringing out the colour of all things;
And soon I knew it came forth from a point—
May I not call it point which was not point,

Having no better word?—translucent, formless,
As though light's very spring that far above
Shone in mid-sky. 'The light of Paradise,
My kinsman,' said the old man; 'our poor peep
Into high heaven.' And as he spoke he smiled.
Well guessed I then that he had borne me sleeping
From the drear rocks outside to where I lay,
And rising stood beside him and looked down
On valley of delight and glittering stream,
And longed that some I knew were with me there.
But as I would have asked in reverend words
Of how, and where, and when, a change came on;
The glitter faded and prismed lustres stole
Down from the centre, till the air seemed waving
With strangest folds of many-coloured light.
And still they faded as in sunset's hour,
Till from beneath us in the darkened glade
There rose a chaunt of voices sweeter far
Than sweetest dream of human harmony.
The words still haunt my ear :

        Maker of light
        With its fair delight,
        Chasing the night
        From Thy young world;
        Who callest day morn
        To the eve first-born,
        Hear us forlorn
        Into night whirled.

Let no guilty mind
Its life's ending find
While with sin entwined
And thoughts of earth;
Grant this, Father dear,
And Thou Son and Peer,
And Love ever near,
God without birth.

' The song thou hearest
Is of the sainted souls who thus in peace
Await the opening of their longed-for home.
They see some thoughts of earth, and good men's
    prayers,
Of all ages and climes to the world's end,
For with keen spirits sense is not as ours,
Though their fond chaunts ascend unto the Lord.
I only in this garden have my flesh,
The rest are purest spirits, yet who see not,
Save in faint symbol and imagining,
That which to see maketh the heaven of man,
Being thus in prison till the times are full;
Their music is the music of the soul
Made vibrate on our hearts by miracle.'
So spake the ancient man, and well I knew
Our father Enoch in his words.   But then
The light again grew stronger, and I saw
The central spring grow brighter in a form,

The form of lamb that lay in death, aud wondered
How such a thing could be, and heard again :

Great God of sacrifice
Whose pains alone suffiee
To open heaven for man,
Wars close upon our way,
Be Thou with us to-day,
Thy banner in the van !

To Him threefold and One,
Be ever honour done,
In whose dear cause we stand ;
Who hath for us in store
His joy for evermore
In our own fatherland.

E'en as they ceased the sign above had changed,
And lo ! like to a dove the fount of rays
Poured a sweet lustre on the happy vale
And all the pleasant risings of the hills ;
And yet again arose the song :

O Holy One, sweet breath of love,
Come down from thy bright reign above
In peace and joy and light ;
Come, Father of the faithful poor,
Come, Giver of the real store,
Come, raptured heart's delight.

Yes, Light of Lights, the Blessed One—
O come, dear Lord, unto Thine own,
Whose bosoms yearn for Thee ;

Without Thy Godhead nothing can
Be an eternal Truth in man
But sin and misery.

Purge Thou that sin from each dull heart,
Thy gentleness of joy impart,
Guide still our weak desires;
That we may serve with steadfast mind
And yet in serving softness find
Made perfect by Thy fires.

Grant to the thought that hath no pride,
The minds that but in Thee confide
Thy seven-fold Spirit's grace;
Grant us to know the endless love,
Grant us to merit Heaven above,
And dying see Thy Face.

The music ceased, and with it half my joy,
Leaving me lost in yearning and amaze.
But even ere my tongue could frame a wish,
My reverend guide began : ' Think not the light,
Which is God's messenger, for ever gleams;
All day the sun shines here as everywhere,
Though still at the hot noons the angel draws
A cloud-curtain across the flaming south
For me and my poor flowers, for I am gardener
As our first father—but enough of this.
Not for vain converse hast thou here been sent,
And with such useless servitor as I;
Rather to nerve thy soul and other souls

Linked with thine own, for a great gain.   The light
Which was an angel's voice, hath shown to thee
The primal mystery.   Ere will was made,
God was for ever in Himself alone,
Yet not alone, for God is love, and love
Must ever love another than oneself
To be all perfect as God still must be.
My son, the Lord is three-fold and yet One.
How we may know in heaven, not even here.'

So spoke the reverend man, and much I wondered,
Yet oft had wondered much how God could be
From ever, He alone, all else created,
Thinking of mighty depths untenanted
In the great desolate past but by His Spirit,
And of His utter loneliness of heart,
And found an answer in this miracle,
As far as thought may sound such awfulness
In Him to whom all may be as one present,
And said : 'O sage, wherefore the lamb all slain
And the bright dove?   What symbols may be
    these?'
And as he answered loved him and his voice.
'The last is love and symbol of God's Spirit,
The lamb of sacrifice and Son of God.
O kinsman ! who would save a sin with life ?'
Such were his words.   ' To thee it has been given

To know the mystery of mysteries;
God sends His own no pain He will not share—
Lo ! now the light !'
                    E'en as he spoke it faded
To the cold lustre of a mighty star,
And slowly moving through the rest, stood still
Above a caverned rock I had not marked,
Nor two beasts standing in the stalls within,
And yet forgot them soon in a bright Child
A woman held, which many men around
Seemed worshipping, while a great chaunt arose
That almost made me faint with joy, though Enoch
Grasped then my hand.   Such Child ! such mother !
    Father,
I cannot speak of them, words are so poor.
Did I say men ?   There were two women there ;
One knelt beside the mother, and her head
Lay on her shoulder as she worshipped weeping,
Yet not with pain I thought—and her bright face
Seemed as a face familiar.   Next to her
Another gazed at me, and she alone,
And woke a strange deep yearning in my joy.
' Behold what is to be and yet what is,'
I heard it whispered then.   'She next the queen,
Captive from Seth, bore two girls to a king,
And died an exile in the land of Cain,
Still calling on the God who is that Child,

The Child and Lamb who Man shall die for sin.
She, too, hath given her babes to do His will.
The other thou hast known in the old years ;
Pray to thy mother, Amos.'   Then I prayed,
And as at prayer of hers the others turned
Infant and queen to me, and straight I swooned,
So keen the sweet joy shot into my heart.
And when I thought again, the star had faded,
And out against the night I saw a cross,
With a pale Man on it that hung in torture,
And knew the Infant I had seen, and fainted
Once more, but not with joy.

               When sense returned,
I lay beside my camel on the rocks,
While Enoch pressed my hand.   ' O friend,' he
   said,
' Our mortal frames scarce bear the angel's voice.
When next thou comest thou shalt be as they,
And yet again with flesh for evermore ;
But never shall a mortal find this garden
As thou, for soon the flood-gates of the deep
Shall open, and yon dawn light it no more.'
And then he breathed a secret in my ear
That is for one, and one alone but me.
And mounting, I came back across the plain,
And met with Seth and her that he had saved,
And so we both are here.

SALEPH.

My children, prayer,
And thankful prayer, will best befit this night,
Whose shades have gathered round us as we heard.
And yet, my daughter, he hath still for thee,
Or I divine untruly, special grace
Reserved.   Go forth, but still remember each;
Though two are dearest all are very dear,
And we shall miss you while you stray.

SCENE III.

The garden outside the cottage.

AMOS and ARVAH.

AMOS.

Not yet—not yet.

ARVAH.

Then tell me how my mother looked—poor mother!

AMOS.

Less like to you than to your sister—yet
Like you.

ARVAH.

Mine is the darker tinge of Cain—
They were together, yours and mine.

M

AMOS.

Together.

Beside the mother and the child.

ARVAH.

The voice,

Or dream, or picture, was for you and me,
And for Hevirah.   Looked she happy, think you?

AMOS.

Both—both—most happy.   Therefore were they
    there,
Not by the cross.

ARVAH.

Hers was sad life on earth

I think I see her weeping as she sits;
You said that she was like Hevirah.

AMOS.

Most like.

ARVAH.

How I shall love her when we meet—and yours.
Now tell me my own secret—I long for it.

AMOS.

I cannot tell you.

ARVAH.

Cannot; you cannot!
Not tell the message that was lent to you,
Aye lent you by the Lord to comfort me.
Of what, then, can it be?

AMOS.

Of thought of yours.

ARVAH.

Of mine! of mine! and yet you tell it not?
I have no thought but might be all your own;
All—all.

AMOS.

I cannot speak it, yet its joy
Has been deep treasured in my inmost heart.

ARVAH.

Now speak, or fare you well, for I go back.

AMOS.

Then thus he said: 'She grieves to lose the earth
Because in heaven all shall be fair as she,
And thou no gainer that thy love is fair.
Tell her in heaven we all shall love the joys
Of others as our own, yet none shall be
To thee so fair except the queen of all.

There are most fair to us who most have served ;
And thou,' so said the sage, ' wert chosen of God
To give His light to her, she His best call
To thee, therefore to the other each most bright.'

ARVAH.

I thank you, friend ; 'tis I should blush, not you—
If that you blush for now I see you not ;
And yet I blush not, nay I glory, Amos ;
The Lord Himself hath loved my little thought,
Thus sending it to you.   Perchance who stand
As we stand now, upon the earth's last verge,
Have keenest insight of His will.   O friend,
Whom God hath joined as He hath joined our hearts,
Must ever find His love in the dear others
Its symbol and its truth.   Were it His will,
I think I would have been good wife to you
Despite my poor Cain's blood—but let that pass.
Think not that I shall flinch.   Watch me to-morrow
If my good sword hew not its honest way
As far as yours—aye yours, call me not comrade,
True comrade, friend and love.   O Amos! Amos!
Yet should I like to live to be your love.
How we would wander down this pleasant slope
On the bright morns where now is blackest night ;
And I could work with you amid your vines,
It were so sweet to live and be together.

AMOS.

Yet should I soon grow old and die perhaps,
And you be lonely on the earth, or I,
Dear love, the Lord hath been most good to us.
When first we two stood thus, you had no hope.

ARVAH.

Alas ! I longed not then to live as now.

AMOS.

And you shall live—witness your own dear message,
And the wise love that reads our inmost hearts.
O could you feel as I felt when I heard
The blessed chaunt ascend unto the Lord,
And saw His angels' light making earth heaven,
Then would you know that love and its best joys,
In flesh but shade, is soul's reality.

ARVAH.

I doubt that I could love more than I love.

AMOS.

Nor I ; but we might have more joy in love,
Deeper capacity for feel of love,
And pleasure in the feel, and over all
More love because more knowledge of our God.
In flesh we faint from pain and faint from joy ;
The vessel is too weak to bear the fire,

And we too blind to reach but in far glimpses
To the eternal beauty, whose wide stars
Are but faint symbol of its endless joy.
Oft wondered I that Abel should be slain,
Who was the friend, not Cain the enemy.
Now wonder thus no more—death is the prize—
Who asks for death Himself doth lead the way;
Therefore are lambs in truest figure slain—
Not ours a death in weakness and reproach,
But thus together hand and hand in joy.
The banner of the Lord waves over us.
You would have died not to betray your girls,
The maidens who had trusted to your strength,
Shall God alone find us untrue?   This longing
For earthly life is but the gift He sends
That He may ask for it from heart to heart.

ARVAH.

My love! my love! tis mine to lean on you;
Perchance were you less strong I were the more—
Who asks for death Himself doth lead the way.
It is a wondrous thought, and yet methinks ——

Enter SETH.

SETH.

How dark it is; I scarce could find you here.
My father longs for both, and bade me seek you;
You'll hear from this Hevirah's song of praise.

ARVAH.

Let us go in.

SETH.

Must we then leave to-morrow?

ARVAH.

To-morrow with the dawn.   Ere night I'll have
Converse with some within.   It well may be
One day might add a victim—aye, or hour.
Kind friends, I thank you both, though well I know
This were but poor reward.   Let us go in.

SCENE IV.

A glade in the mountains over the city of Cain.

SETH, AMOS, and HEVIRAH.

SETH.

He knows one will return.
I lingered with him till your forms grew faint,
Still thinking he might change, but he changed not.
I never marked before how like you are;
His was your very look upon the sands
When once again he blessed me and I came.

AMOS.

His prayers will follow us.

SETH.

      Do you remember
How almost on this spot I longed that God
Would send us down with club and sword to smite
The evil ones below? And now He sends us.
Perhaps our fancies oft are shadows given
Of that which is to come.

HEVIRAH.

      Lo! how the fires
Begin to light the smoke upon the mountain.

SETH.

This morn, ere yet the dawn showed in the east,
I saw from our sheepfold the same strange light
Upon the central range as on the night
You slew the panther, Amos, by their sleep.

AMOS.

All day the mountain was in labour. Hark!
The sounds again!

SETH.

    There go the stones, I ween;
No pleasant neighbour is that mountain-dome

To your close streets, Hevirah.   Have you seen
Often such blaze as lit the skies that night ?

HEVIRAH.

Never before.   Yet were there tales of streams
Of molten rock poured out in the old times.

SETH.

They are stout men, those sons of Cain, to sin
Under the very fire-scourge of the Lord
Poised in mid air for vengeance.   Must we slay
All that this day shall give into our power ?

AMOS.

Until the maidens are more strong than they.
Then not another life.   Such is the will
Of Arvah.

HEVIRAH.

    All but one.   O spare the head
That wears a crown.

AMOS.

    That, too, is wish of hers.

SETH.

If all were slain, the race should have an end,
Or sons of God wive with the girls of Cain.

AMOS.

Methinks the Lord regards less Cain or Seth
Than the true will of each more earnest heart.
But see, where Arvah comes.

HEVIRAH.

                    With bended brow
And arrows rattling as she strides.   Something
Hath angered her beyond her wont—and lo!
The smoke, upfolding, almost hides the day.

Enter ARVAH.

ARVAH.

Quick! quick! there is no moment to be lost.
But yesterday another met her death,
Deep-wronged.   She was of ours, taken by force,
And leaped into the chasm calling for vengeance.
The rest e'en now huddle together armed,
Fearing an instant raid.   Beside the gate
The chief sage stood, with many a greybeard else,
Watching for me.   She almost had her wish,
Poor Leah!

AMOS.

Thou hast not slain him?

ARVAH.

                    No—and yet
The good shaft touched my ear.   Let us go on!

The secret pass is open still.   When deeds
Like these are done, God well may bid us smite
And die.

HEVIRAH.

Lo now the fire ! the fire !

SETH.

By heaven

It is a fearful sight.

AMOS.

Still, still, it mounts.

The trees grow lurid, as upon the night
When first you fled.

ARVAH.

As best befits our purpose.

The day is dead, but in my brain the moans
Of tortured wretches drown yon natural throes.
Amos, we go together to the end,
Hevirah ever near.   Let us not think,
But strike—or think of wrongs—'twas almost here
We met first, you and I.   Seth with his good sword
Will lead the weaker bands, and God for all.
Let us go down.

SCENE V.

A lower slope of the mountain.

SETH and HEVIRAH.

HEVIRAH.

Set me down here.   The smoke is past,
And I can breathe, speak, almost think again.
There, on that mossy bank.   O Seth, the glare,
The hideous glare! And still my ears are ringing
With the hoarse shrieks worse than thy dream.
   Alas!
It is most terrible to die in sin
And pain.   Forgive me that I thank thee not
My brother, my dear brother—thou art unwounded;
And yet thy locks are singed and garments seared,
So near the breath of an avenging God.
Yes, I can think again.   We two are left
A little while—I but a little while.
Where is my sister ?   Nay, I read the answer.
Yet tell me all, O friend !   I have no thought
Till I was in thine arms, and could not breathe,

Stifled with fire and smoke. I lay behind
When I was hurt, until the horror came.

SETH.

Lean on me thus, and I will tell, or try.
We still pressed on in our first rush until
Thy father's gates were almost gained ; but there
The gathering numbers held their own, and soon
Bore us back inch by inch. Arrows were useless
In the thick press, and our light weights should
    yield
By slow degrees to greater strength. Then heard I
Thy Arvah bid the rearmost fall behind
And use their bows, and soon the arrows flew
From the flat roofs like hail over our heads,
And strengthened by their wounds we kept our
    ground.
Amos and Arvah on the one side fought,
And axe and sword together hewed their way
Until again the gates were almost reached,
When a huge man, bearing a mighty rock,
Broke staggering through and heaving fell on her
And bore her to the ground, and ere she rose
A javelin pierced her, and she fell with Amos,
Struck as he leaned to aid. Then came to me
A strength that was not mine, and I smote down

The swords that crossed me like weak wands, and
  clave
The giant to the chin, and once again
Felt the Archangel held his shield over me.
I saw our Amos and your sister smile
To be amongst their friends, as hand in hand
They died. I saw them smile, just saw them
  once.
There was a lurid glow on all things then ;
Upon the wicked eyes before me and the swords,
Yet none might look up to the sky, so fierce
And swift the rain of blows, until the arrows
No more came from behind, but screams of death.
Then thought I of my father and his fate,
When lo ! the roar as of a thousand waters,
And blaze as of a thousand lightnings, fell
Before me and around, and a great shriek,
As in my dream that night, and all was fire.
I scarce can tell the rest ; the streets are hell,
And yet but few of ours are touched. The moun-
  tain
Was the good sword of God.

HEVIRAH.

                       Pray for them, pray,
Thou and thy father in the quiet fields.
Again the smoke is blinding me—not smoke,

It is not smoke.   O brother, I must go.
See, Arvah calls me.   I am going, Seth.
Thy hand, thy hand.   And Amos and the Child.
His hands are red ; 'tis as thy father said—
The sin is past for ever.

A LEGEND OF THE SEINE.

———◦◦◦———

PART I.

         A STORY I read long ago ;
A little simple tale of simple times,
When men had stronger hearts than now. To me
There is a beauty in its faithfulness,
A beauty and a truth for evermore.

In a grey tower that gloomed above the Seine
Lived the last son of a seigniorial race ;
Ungraceful, stubborn, rude, and hard of hand,
That in its walls had citadel'd their strength,
And worse than strength, for many an age. A youth,
Scarce yet a man, silent and solitary,
Who roamed through the dark woods, his single
   wealth,
Or sate him by the rugged river-side,
Too proud to seek the converse of his peers,
Too proud to mingle with the sullen serfs,

Too proud to work, or learn, or aught but feel,
And hate the sluggish current of his life.
And yet, at times, when the clear moon looked down
Upon the pallid splendours of the night,
And from his chamber far above he watched
The waters quivering on under her beam—
The waters that he loved, if he loved aught—
Or when the great strong sun, that king of earth,
Poured out a golden glory o'er the land,
And through the liquid crystal of those waves
He cleft his manly way, he too felt joy;
Keener perchance than most men know—a joy
In nature and his own strong self. Oft, too,
Amid the summer softness of the woods
He dreamed bright dreams and knew that they were
    bright,
And loved them well and found a listener soon:
Ada, the great Count's daughter. He who owned
Near half a province and the whole King's ear—
Young Albert's neighbour—but who loved not him
Nor his. And yet his daughter often strayed
Now through that neighbour's woodlands with her
    maids,
And met him oft by chance, and felt ere long
There was a brighter freshness in the green,
A gentler wooing in the summer air,
A sweet strange burst of gladness o'er the earth;

Until her sire, dark-frowning, bade her bound
Her wanderings with his lands, and she obeyed.

And ere long knights and plumes and pennons high,
And all the armèd pomp of feudal state,
Swept upwards to the castle of the Count,
While on the plain beneath, level and strong,
Rose the wide lists, and it was noised afar,
'The best lance wins great glory and a sword;'
Or as some put it, 'A most glorious sword,
With yellow ducats massed upon its hilt.'
And each good knight looked to his armour-straps,
And to the feeding of his trusted steed;
Till one bright morn they strove till sunny noon
In noble emulation horse and man.
By then two Sirs lay senseless in their tents,
And four were scarcely better off, if better;
And all the people were in cheerful mood,
Feeling, good souls! that as the gentle blood
Grew rich on all the fat things of the earth,
'Twas fair to see its colour now and then.
But by that hour of noon a single knight
Stood matched against all comers, but none came;
A very Paladin of knights, and no
More came till, as the gazers waxed cross,
A single plume waved darkly through the trees—
An old dull plume, o'er arms as old and dull—

But larger far than had been seen that day.
Slowly the rider came across the ground,
And slowly gave his challenge: 'Nameless I;
If this Sir wants a tilter, here I stand.'
'Nameless, you win no prize.'   'So be it—mine,
Why throw it to the dogs or serfs.'   So spake he,
And they who heard him liked him not.   But then
Our Paladin pulled down his helmet's face,
And from the high pavilion came a breath
Of favour feminine.   So brave a knight,
So courteous too, while not a creature knew
That other person in the queer old steel!
And yet when like two great bulls iron-cased
They crashed upon each other, lance and lance,
It was the Paladin who reeled, but kept
His seat, yet not the favour on his crest,
That, idly fluttering, slowly sought the ground;
A knot of blue—the colour Ada loved.
As they passed on, some said a baleful fire
Flashed from the stranger's vizor, and all saw
He loosed his steel axe in its hold, like one
Who thinks him of a trusted friend.   Meanwhile
With all the common's love of common gifts
The people cheered him, till with largess-cry
Some small boys met him, but he passed along
Unheeding.   Then, the tide of favour changing,
All prophesied a fall; but he fell not,

Shaking our Paladin again most shrewdly.
A third encounter, and this time the great knight
Drove his fresh horse—a lumbering Flemish horse—
Full on the stranger, and his mare went down,
Not he.   All saw him on his feet and then,
A lightning flash of steel, and horse and man
The conqueror went backwards, with a cleft
Six inches deep between those Flemish ears,
And then from all the heralds, guards, and crowd,
Went up one cry of horror at foul blow,
And all rushed shouting in—but first the Count;
Up went the stranger's vizor, and they saw
A young flushed face, broad, savage, lion-like—
But not more savage than the great Count's joy:
' Now yield thee, churl, till that my varlets whip
Thee armless from the lists—that is the doom.'
And then o'er Albert's soul—for it was he—
Came the old longing of his Northern sires,
To rush on madly, slaying to be slain ;
Came, too, a stronger thought, ' And be the sport
Of yonder perfumed fools, like a quelled boar ;'
And leaning one hand on his risen mare—
His trembling mare—a hand that seemed to say
' 'Twas not thy fault, old lady'—he sprang up
Wrong-sided as he was, and urged her on.
And then the outward crowd—the small boys most—
Yelled ' Churl ! out, churl ! out ! out !' but not a
    hand

Was laid upon his rein—for some there were
Who liked him for his deeds—as he passed on.

On through the Autumn trees, where mocking birds
Chattered their jibes, while darkly drop by drop
The mare's slow blood lay on the leaves behind;
On by the rock-bound margin of the hill
Into the deeper tangled alder-wood,
Where great brown hemlocks withered by the path;
On foot at last, up the hard slippery track
That slowly mounting through dark firs caught
   sounds
Of surging waters and the downward roar
Of the great river, borne on the breeze;
Then out upon the flat rock o'er the fall
The rock above the cold swift-moving depths
Of currents sweeping onward to the fall,
Like runners gathering strength before a leap—
The fall that many an ancient line foretold
Was bound up with the fortunes of his race.
Oft had he stood tranced in its roar, wondering
How this could be; but now he wondered not.
He was the last—the last of all his blood—
And well he knew, for he had scanned it well
On summer noons, one boulder shaken there,
And the weak dam was gone for evermore.
'Twas said a demon passing woman fair

Lurked in the whirl beneath, and played with souls;
That she could lure and daunt, and daunting damn;
But if man's courage braved her there but once,
Her spells were gone for ever.   Such the tale
As he thought of it then—thought of it long;
Then mounting, past into the sea of woods
That swelled in many a wave to the far tower.
Standing out dark against the evening sky,
Like some grim giant, desolate, but strong.

An evil spot.   The peasant homeward bound,
As he sped by it shuddering in the night,
Would dream he heard faint shrieks ring through
  the air,
Far echoes of a more than mortal pain;
And thinking of old tales, of deeds done once,
And cries of agony from living flesh,
Would cross himself and speed the more.
                                        That eve,
From out the central chamber of the keep
A dim light shone, and all night through a step
Smote dully on the great old arched floor
Backwards and forwards, while a human heart
Fought with, not conquering, the hell within—
A man's—baptised that day in pain a man—
And yet ere morning broke, scarce human still.
Upon the rough oak table lay a lock

Of light brown hair, tied with a knot of blue;
Thrice had he seized it, as a man will seize
Some venom'd thing to crush it with his heel.
But still it lay unscathed—a light brown lock,
With just a golden glimmer in its sheen,
Faint as the last weak good within himself,
The flush of strife throbbed through his veins no
 more;
That eagerness of strength that made all things
Seem possible; but still the longing grew
E'en with the ebbing of his dying hopes—
That strongest, deadliest—to give back
Scorn for scorn and blow for blow—till peace, youth,
 life,
Seemed but as feathers weighed against that hope —
Hope fading ever more.   The veriest serf
Was not more powerless than he.   His sires—
His rough strong sires—would flout his bones at last.
As powerless as a serf!   Yes, he might dog
His rival's path and slay him from a ditch—
Serfs can do this—and she would wed another,
And tell him the sad story as he toyed
With all that wealth of hair.   Oh for the right
To call it his while her grim father smiled,
Then spurn it from his heart for ever.   *That*
Were joy—and could naught give it? Were there not
Powers invisible that do the things

Beyond all hope and likelihood to man?
Oft had he dreamed of such, but ne'er till now
With longing.   Then he paused—a sudden thrill
Smote to the very marrow of his bones—
In all the darksome corners of the room
No form had risen, yet he felt a will
Had converse with his own, and feeling, stood
Half trancèd in his keen expectancy.
'Give me thy soul, and thou shalt have thy wish.'
'And be thy slave?—never!'   Was it a dream
That laughter mocking o'er his head 'Already.'
'I am no slave, false spirit; what I will
I do.'   'Well spoken; be my friend—no slave.'
He heard no sound, but deep he felt the words;
And then a short gust from the window shook
The light lock, and it fell; and gazing outwards,
Far off—on the bare hill—he saw the moon look down
With a strange burst of light upon the stones
Where Druid priests had held their rites of old.
'In one year from her marriage bring her there.
Is it a bargain?'   'Take my oath.   It needs not.'
And lo! when downward leaning he would seek
The ravished lock, although he searched and searched
He found it not, but felt a jibe again:
'It is my *earnest*, friend; our bargain's struck.
So far thy will is mine.'

                                    Within an alcove
Upon the turret stairs, in a rude niche,
There stood and smiled the Blessed Maid and Child—
A gracious statue, that his mother loved.
Her last faint words besought her son to fill
Her place, and tend with his own hands the lamp
Beneath; and he had promised and obeyed.
But now, when the gray dawn made all things
    ghastly—
But ghastliest his own young haggard face—
It barely glimmered, for the dregs of oil
Were low within, as dries a summer pool.
He saw it as he passed—yet passed—but stood
One moment at the turn and doubted; then
Returning, sought the flask and filled; yet looked
Not upwards, where a smile had seemed to steal
Over the faces with the growing light—
The one bright thing in all that gloomy place.

PART II.

'Joy! joy!   Pile up the beacons on the hills!
Smooth all the causeways—from the topmost turret
Fling out the brave old banner of his House!
The old red cross that never never sank.
Let white-robed maidens meet them on the road,

Pure as his fame and joyful as our hearts.
He comes—our knight- -the foremost lance of all ;
Our own good knight. From Orleans to the Somme
We've driven the Islanders, field after field,
Grim as their bull-dogs when the tiger springs,
Back to their holds, along the western sea.;
And of them all, counts, princes, and the rest
Was none like him—not one except the Maid,
And she——'' Hush! speak not of her! let her name
Be in our hearts not on our lips—curse them!
She was our sister, and they left her lorn ;
They used her as they use us all—but he,
He would have died for her—that's why we love him.
I tell ye, masters, from the hour he woke
Out of his fever-trance and knew her taken,
He hath not smiled—not once—not by the altar,
I marked him well. Sir Albert never smiled—
Not when his young bride, like our vines at dawn,
In the soft pride of her unclouded love,
Looked up and blushed, first leaning on his arm,
His brow was dark as ever. He hath sworn,
'Tis said, to make a brand from Rouen light
A fire beyond the seas will flicker far.'
' And if he has he'll keep his oath ; though, faith,
I'd hold a raid among those Northerns like
Putting one's hand into a hornet's nest ;
But he knows best.' ' How aged he is ; who'd think

It was the youth who used to wander mooning
Along the river here ; and yet at night
He oft roves forth alone, and spends whole days
Listening to minstrels when he finds them.'   ' 'Tis
A taste inherited : in the far south
E'en now his uncle Count, whose spears he led,
Childless and old, harps many a tale of love.'
' Good faith, a curious fancy ; our old Sirs
Had made short work of harpers and such like.
But come ! the seneschal may want us ; come ! '

So gossipped Albert's peasant warriors
The morn he and his bride, the great Count's
    daughter,
Came first a wedded pair to the old tower.

'Twas evening, and the two had wandered long
Through the deep woods, she hailing each old spot
That had for her new tale of love—he cold
And passionless, as was his wont—till now
The clear sun shone in through the outer trees,
A central disk in a great web of light ;
And on them moving outwards, and the path
And the broad stems, fell the soft lustrous glow
Until her fair face, like a sweet saint's shone,
Seen down cathedral aisles.

                                     Upon the verge
Of the descent they stood watching the river,
Swollen by Autumnal floods.   Far off the plain,
Spread out like a great map, with many a lake
Bent by the circling waters ; and o'er all
The witchery of the evening hour.   'Here stay we,'
She whispered, 'till the sun goes down.   Albert,
I am so happy;' and he stayed; and whispering still,
So close his face she leaning, she told him
The thoughts of that long walk—how, when of old
They met, there had been thorns in all the joy—
Fears for her right-doing and her father's wrath—
And when the ruin came and all was misery,
She felt it was her earning—but now all
Was bright again.   God had forgiven her,
God and her own Saint Genevieve.   She feared not
To tell him now all this, for she had seen
Our Lady on the stairs, and his old lamp,
And Martha told on him ; but she would tend
The light henceforth, and do his mother's bidding ;
For being wife, she was himself.'   So prattled she,
Half toying with his cap the while ; but he
Sat listening till the great West glowed all red.
Then rising suddenly, he cried, 'It is on fire!
I cannot bear it ! come!' and she sprang up,
Her little face all whitened with the pain
Of that strange fierceness.   'Bear with me,' he said,

As he strode on among the darker trees;
' I'm not myself at times.   My mother's blood
Boils into frenzy—'tis our privilege—all bards
And madmen—bear with me: I hate that glow,
That sunset glow of fire.'   And then she thought—
For she had lain upon his breast six moons,
And all her thoughts were his—she thought he
    dreamed
Of his old comrade and her lurid pain.
And leaning closer to his side she breathed
' You loved her so—I would have loved her too.
O speak of her! please speak! it breaks my heart
You will not speak to me.   You once would say
You'd like to have a secret to tell me.
Speak to me, Albert.   You have no sister,
I no brother ; speak as my brother now.'

So pleaded she, but he half savagely
Made answer, ' Child, a devil I—— poor child !
A thriving devil of some odd years' growth—
And thou hast married me, that is the joke !
Think not it is my pain for that dead saint—
Though that is much—that makes me—well, like
    this.
I never loved but thee—not as a man
Loves woman ; but since that accursed tilt,
And I, fool, deemed thee false, I have been mad
Or devil-sold, I know not which.'   So spake he,

And as he spake the heart beside him leaped
In its great joy.   'He never loved but me!
But me—he never loved but me! oh joy! oh joy!'
'I loved her as you loved your saints, that's all;
And she loved me, since from a Paris ditch
I bore her in my arms, and spake of France
And of the people's wrongs; and times to come
She saw oft in her dreams, when from the Rhine
To the great Southern snows all men shall be
Free, equal, brothers, in this land of ours;
And I would hear as if an angel spoke.

'One night I could not sleep; 'tis my disease,
And wandering forth amid our tents that rose
All ghost-like o'er the plain, I strayed at last
Into a forest path that crossed the woods
Upon our flank.   Oft paused I, listening
Lest English scouts should lurk among the trees;
But nought saw I or heard, till where two roads
Met, in the centre, by a cross there lay
All prostrate at its feet, with twining arms,
A woman's form in woman's agony.
E'en as I stood amazed, irresolute,
It bent back to its knees as with a spasm
Of pain that mastered all the frame; and then,
Above the white clasped hands I saw the face.
Ada, it was the Maid! she I'd seen break

Like a young Pallas through the shivering spears,
Smiling the while ; 'twas she had lain before me,
Writhing as a bruised worm.   ' Ah not the fire !
Dear Lord, not fire.   My life for France, but spare
The pain of fire ! I'm woman still.'   And then,
Ada, a deep low wail of bitter pain—
That makes me half fiend now to think that men
Still live that tortured her—passed through the trees.
But even as I heard I saw, or thought
I saw—what do we see, what think we see ?—
A change come o'er the Dead Christ on the Cross.
It may be that the moon looked clearer forth,
But every nerve and sinew seemed to start
From the stretched form in one great frozen pang,
Till like a gentle death-sleep o'er her frame
Passed a great rest as there she knelt, and all
Was still.

   Ada, that cry rang through my ears
The day my squires upheld me as I rode
Our last day's ride on Rouen.   It was evening
Ere yet we gained the wood fronting the town,
Some thrice a hundred spears, good men and true.
I whimpered like a child in the keen joy
That France and she had still three hundred friends—
The brave old fated number.   In the gate
A peasant's cart entangling was to free
Our passage.   There, you know the rest.   I grow

A babbler ; till the last eternal doom
Shrieks evermore ' *Too late!* '—a babbler still.
Lo! my old cot! Come, be a boatman's bride,
And skim over that rush one hour with me.'

So spake he, pointing to the swollen stream,
A glitter in his eye she knew but loved not ;
Nor loved the eddying waves, but dared to die.
Die ! what was death to her for his dear love ?
Or fire, ten fires ; she would have braved them all.
And when he pushed the skiff against the land,
Put out her little foot upon the seat,
Firm as her own St. Genevieve ; but he
Flung off into the stream scarce heeding her,
With a fierce hatred in him of his life
And most things good ; and all the waters rushed
Circling and surging into eddying whirls
Around them, as the bark swept fragile on
With strong swift urges, as an autumn leaf
Will flicker o'er a stream descending still,
For ever near and nearer came the roar
Of the great fall. She knew he mocked at all,
And played with the grim waters as a rider
With a fresh steed, scanning the distance still,
While the tinged light fell on his swaying form
And all its latent strength ; but in his eye
Was still the glitter that she loved not well,

But loved to soothe, and would soothe by-and-bye,
With the soft pleadings of her harp, she thought,
A little David to her Saul. And then,
Despite the rushing waters and the fear,
She smiled at her own modesty, that made
Her simple self like the great poet king.
But even then, in the mid stream of all,
The flitting skiff edged sideways on an end,
A sharp cut end, of a great stranded tree,
That lurked below, and with a sudden turn
She felt the cold waves splashing round her eyes,
And could not scream ; felt, too, a strong hand seize
Her head and bear her up, and knew ere long
Her arms were round her Albert, and he strove
For shore, for shore ; oh could he win the shore ?
She felt the energy of strength that seemed
Half winning, but the rush that swept them down
Grew swifter every stroke.   Oh might he win !
He could have answered her ' No, just too late.'
Too late ! *too late !* what was it he had said
But now ?   The shriek of everlasting doom,
' *Too late !* '   Aye, fire for evermore ! the fire
The Maid had shrank from, his for evermore.
Curse on that clinging tunic ! Were he free,
His strong limbs free, e'en now he'd gain the shore.
Who laughed ?—aye they may laugh for ever now—
Oh for one minute of his naked self,

One minute's unimpeded strife for life ;
For life, for time ; time to repent, yes time.
' Quick ! fling her off ! yes, fling her off ! quick !
 quick !
Both cannot live, and she's a saint ; and you—'
' Am that which still can master you, foul fiend !
Whate'er my fate, I die *a man.*' Then Ada
Felt that his efforts slackened, and she knew
He husbanded his strength for the great fall,
And on one little hand beneath his breast
She felt his laid all lovingly, and said
To her own heart, ' Oh joy, he thinks of me !
Of me ! Oh joy. Help him, St. Genevieve,
Not me, not me ; but save him in this strait ! '
And even as she prayed she seemed to see,
Through all the waters and the splash and roar,
A sweet pale light upon the land afar,
And thought it was the chapel on the hill,
And thought no more.

     But he, still husbanding
His strength, steered straightly on, with a strange
 joy
Within his heart, like one who wins. In front
He saw the huge tree's boughs borne onward fast
Behind the frail bark that unmoored its strength ;
Saw, too, the circling curl of the great fall
And all the strife beyond. When lo ! the tree,

Just as it reached the ledge, seemed upward swung,
And with a roar that echoed many a mile
The mass of pent-up waters forward heaved
Over the broken bar—the dam had yielded;
And like two leaves, up, down, along, around,
But ever clasped, closer and closer clasped,
Through all the darkness and the whirl and race,
One senseless and the other scarce alive,
The two lay on a field at last.

PART III.

AND now the winter darkened all the land,
A dim, drear, murky winter, blackening
The great arms of the trees, and drip by drip
Soddening the chill earth and the thoughts of men.
A joyless leaden air hung o'er the earth.
The fogs clung to it like a gathered shroud;
The uncheered beasts pined in the sickly fields.
No glow of sunshine lit the noonday woods;
No breeze frost-laden stirred the crisping leaves.
The blessed snow fell not. All things were dull,
And dank, and desolate; and Ada knew
The heart she loved grew darker day by day;
Dark beyond reach of her and her poor love,
And all her little arts and winning ways,

Deeper and deeper in the unfitful gloom
Of a cold blank despair. He knew his fate,
For he was one who thought till all things fitted,
Or seemed to fit. Some power, not of himself,
Upon their marriage-day's recurring morn,
Would take him and his bride to that far hill;
And then his reason failing utterly,
The reason he had used to make such compact,
His own doomed hand would strike the fatal blow,
And slay her that he loved, thence wandering forth
A horror evermore. Such were his dreams,
That grew like certainties as still he dreamed.
Yes, fate was fate—the very river bed
Had yielded to that fate lest he should die,
And thus his doom evade. So thought he now.
At first he deemed the ancient prophecy
Fulfilled, and he a conqueror; but now
None but dark fancies reigned within his heart.
He could not pray—he dared not, would not, pray—
Till one night dreaming as he ever dreamed,
Weird vivid dreams, but this, strangest of all,
He thought he wandered in a bright warm land
Beside blue waves that rippled to his feet,
Until he gazed upon a woman's face
In a low chamber; a pale face, beautiful
Beyond all thought of man, but sadder far
Than beautiful, and yet so beautiful,

Its pain was like a glory.   She looked straight
Through a small door, at what he could not see,
Could see naught but the beauty of that face,
The beauty and the woe—until it grew
Like one familiar to him.   Then he saw
The other chamber, and a Boy that played
There with some wood, the remnants of men's work.
Two laths were nailed together in a cross
And fixed against the wall, and He still watching
    them,
Saw not His mother's face, or so it seemed,
Till suddenly He turned, and sprang to her
In radiance of strange smile, and tried to kiss
Away the tears and all the woe.   But lo!
The pale face could not move in its great pain;
And then a deeper light lit the young eyes,
A light of love unutterable, Godlike,
And even as a teacher spake the Son—
'My mother I have asked, and it is given,
Through all the years, no one shall turn to thee
With his whole heart, and be unheard of God.'

Then Albert woke, but still the blessed words
Rang in his ears, 'No one shall turn to thee
And be unheard;' and springing to his feet,
He stole out to the alcove on the stairs,
And saw that face again in the pale light,

And prayed before it where his mother prayed
In the old times.   Prayed prostrate for long hours,
And so each night, and Ada never woke.
But when the fatal morn had risen, they went
Together, she upon her palfrey riding,
He walking by her side, up towards the hills.
And when they neared the chapel on the hill,
She thinking of the light over the fall,
Went in and prayed, and he, worn out it may be,
With his long wakefulness, sat down and slept,
Until his wife returning, they went on.
On toward the great huge stones upon the heath,
He still as in a dream, and wondering
What thing might happen next; and yet he seemed
To see all things that he had done more plainly,
And all the love that had been given him;
But still half in amazement went his way
Unto the outer circle of the stones;
Then she beside him left her horse, and stood
At last upon the central stone of all—
The altar-stone.   And lo! a great snake writhed
Out from beneath, and hissing, made at her.
And Albert saw her face, and wondered more,
Incapable of motion or of word;
But knew it was not Ada that had laid
Her firm foot on the serpent's head, who coiled,
And writhed, and foamed, and then was still.

While from the sky, and air, and hill, and plain,
Went up one mighty cry of jubilee,
As from a thousand thousand voices : ' Hail,
O Mary ! Mother ! Tower of David, hail !"

And he awoke.   She stood beside him.   Ada,
His wife ; all smiling at his sleep.   So fair,
So fair, oh never half so fair before.
' We will not go on ; I have slept,' he said,
' And had a dream, a strange dream, while you
    prayed.'
And then they journeyed back.   And all the birds—
'Twas almost Spring—were chanting in the trees,
And the sweet sunshine glittered o'er the earth ;
And from the peasants' homes the smoke curled
    cheerily
Before the mid-day meal.   But all his mind
Could hold but just one thought that she was there,
And she was his.

                        That evening, as he stirred
An ancient volume, seeking for a tale
Of Christian saintliness, something that lay
Upon it fell.   It was a light brown lock,
Tied with blue ribbon.

THE LADY CLOTILDE.[1]

PART I.

THE lady Clotilde was the heiress of Lyle ;
She owned its broad grass-lands for many a mile,
For many a long reach of headland and bay,
O'er valley and down to the hills far away.
      She was lord of the ' pays,'
      And had ' waifs' and ' estrays,'
And 'flotsam' and 'jetsam,' as somebody says,
Which might really mean something perhaps in her
  days.
      And then she was pretty,
      And wickedly witty—
There *were* people no doubt who thought that was a
  pity—
But every one said through the length of these isles

---

[1] This tale was begun many years ago, in an attempt to imitate what is perhaps inimitable.

You'd not meet such prime wheatland or see such
 arch smiles
As the lady Clotilde's, the fair heiress of Lyle's.

Now these were the days of romance that I write of,
When your mere fortune-hunting was thought poorly
 quite of;
   So I need scarcely say
   That when every day
Young gentlemen rode up to fair Castle Lyle,
Arrayed at all points in the most reckless style,
None thought of the wheatlands but all of the smile;
And when the great Countess of Knares wrote cares-
 sing,
'Her most gentle cousin,' so charmingly pressing
The bright little maid to that stronghold again,
'Thy playmate, son Guy, will be home with us
 then.'
The good lady ne'er thought of her ample domain;
   Not she—nor young Vere,
   Nor the Sieur de Boremere,
Nor Eustace, nor Scroope, nor Sir Marmaduke Grey,
Who had lost his first wife, and was just getting
 grey,
Nor any, indeed, but stout Hugh de Launay,
Whose lands by the side of the fair Clotilde's lay,
And who always told truth in a very rude way.

But there by the score
At least, if not more,
They kept flirting, and drinking, and sighing, and
dressing,
And singing, and tilting, and dining, and pressing,
Until most of them finding the thing would not do,
They quietly held on and watched one or two ;
For the prophecies soon pretty evenly fell
Between Brian de Aylmar and Ralf de Lavelle.

Young Ralf de Lavelle was short and thin,
His back curved out and his chest curved in,
And he said bitter things with a sneering grin,
A curl of the lip and a mocking eye,
(When men called him names he was not by).
Till many who liked the 'outrance' pretty well,
Would grow pale at the sight of that Ralf de
Lavelle.

Now I've said that beside being uncommonly pretty,
The Lady Clotilde was uncommonly witty ;
And, of course, if there's one thing on earth that's a
bore,
It's to see your neat joke fall uncaught to the floor ;
To have to explain
'What is it you mane.'
As I *have* heard it put (though to give us our due,

If men throve upon wit we'd be fat enough too).
Now Scroope, and De Vere, and Sir Marmaduke
   Grey,
Though very nice men, had not got much to say ;
And though they tried hard to laugh loud when they
   ought to,
It was at the wrong times just as often as not too.
       But young master Ralf,
       With a bantering laugh,
Being ever and always it seemed in the vein,
Would give her her neat little ' mots ' back again,
       Still capping each jest
       With better and best,
Until for five minutes it would not be all over,
So sure for her ' Roland ' was always his ' Oliver ; '
       And, indeed, I must say,
       He was pleasant and gay,
With the ladies he liked as became a true knight,
Though with men he was always unbearable quite,
       Still poking his fun
       At his friends everyone ;
But ever on Aylmar his worst he would try,
For there often was something which glanced in *his*
   eye,
The wit felt was danger, and loved to defy.

Alas ! we who live in degenerate days,

When such poor things as learning and arts have
    their praise,
And muscle though still a redoubtable name
Is not quite the one opening left us to fame,
Can scarce fancy their lot in those times, to whom
    fate
Gave a mind for aspiring, but not twelve stone
    weight.
        I think I may tell
        Of poor Ralf de Lavelle,
That if Madame Nature had done well her part,
And given him a body as stout as his heart,
His powers of word-hitting had never been known,
Or been kept for the things which deserved them
    alone.

By the way no one knew that Sir Brian at all,
Except as a broad-shouldered knight good and tall,
Who at many a tilting before Clotilde Lyle,
Had sent them all spinning in quite 'tip top' style.
It was said he had been the sworn friend of her
    brother,
(Who was killed before Acre, or somewhere or
    other),
And all knew that often, when going away,
He'd been asked in the most pressing manner to
    stay.

Indeed, people said—but then what won't they say !—
Still everyone saw his dark eyes ever bent
Toward her bright girlish form wherever it went ;
And some people thought that when he would be by
Their hostess was often more silent and shy
   Than became a young lady
   Who had broken already
More hearts by her smiles, and her wiles, and her
  miles
Of deep grass-land, than anyone else in these isles.

At last, one fine night, in the old Castle Hall
They'd a ' rout,' or a dance, or what we'd call a ' ball ;'
And indeed, on third thoughts, some will have it, I
  see,
That all stopped in the house, so things don't quite
  agree ;
But never before had the fair maid of Lyle
Been so radiant of look or so graceful of smile.
True ' largesse ' of beauty, all round her they fell,
But none got so much quite as Ralf de Lavelle ;
   While he, on his part
   Grew smart and more smart,
And chasséed and gibed in his very best way,
Until everyone thought he had made famous play,
   And must win ere long,
   But I think they were wrong.

For court'sying at last as a fairy-queen may,
·She motioned her partner to lead her away
      To a tall arm-chair,
      And leaning there
With his plumed cap on the wide seat thrown,
Stood Brian de Aylmar, pale and alone.

      Well, they danced that night
      Till the grave moonlight
Peep'd in in a way that was shocking quite,
Making every young lady look just ' like a fright,'
Making long ghastly windows, that did not seem
   ' right,'
Glare up pale and cold on the tapestry's height ;
For the candles were all burning down to their
   ends,
With a spluttering protest that weakly offends,
And the Cyprus was finished, and pale Malvoisie,
And the young men had taken to raw eau-de-vie,
      A thing it is said
      That soon gets to the head,
So the ladies said ' Good night,' and went to bed.

The bright sun is rising on fair Castle Lyle—
The sheen of its mere you might see for a mile—
And milkmaids, and larks, and all live things are
   glad,

For Nature—— Alas! at description I'm bad.
       So all fine lines scorning,
       Without more adorning,
I'll just tell you at once it's a very fine morning.
In the western tower Sir Marmaduke Grey
Has lamented o'er every fresh hair that's grown grey;
But even he now is just ready, they say.
All the rest have been down for this hour and a half,
Save *one*.   What on earth has become of Sir Ralf?
       Its nine—its eleven
       (They had breakfast at seven),
But still by the side of that gentleman's door
       In the long corridor,
His boots and hot water are laid on the floor.
       He must be there still—
       Perhaps he is ill.
       They knock.   No reply,
       And they wonder why.
At last they go in with a push of the door,
And they see a smooth bed, and they see nothing
   more;
And they search through the woods, and they search
   through the park,
       Till it's quite getting dark;
When at last on the sea-beach his mantle is found,
And everyone's sure he fell in and was drowned.

Why, what a thing is life ! To-day
We eat, drink, work, scheme, sell, or pay,
In some great instances—our bills.
We lock our hearts up and our tills,
And while the funds rise we've been buying—
Just as she's melted by our sighing—
Nay, even while our book is read
And *paid for*—we—why we are dead.
And yet if life be, as it is,
A seed-time given to harvest bliss ;
If every deed and word and thought
May be again before us brought,
With countless-fold of increase given
In the infinity of heaven ;
If every human act of ours
Through all the idle ling'ring hours
Is of such wondrous destiny
That it shall last ; when all we see—
All this great matter-world around—
Earths upon earths to the mind's bound,
Is lost in nothingness again,
Alas ! to live is *fearful* then !

Now whether they thought this of poor Ralf Lavelle,
I really don't know, so I really can't tell ;
But I think I may say, with slight chance of being
    wrong,

If they did, that such thoughts did not trouble
    them long.
        Though, indeed, Clotilde Lyle
        Was not seen to smile
For a week, at the least, and a week's a long while.
And ere that was passed, there had happened instead
Enough to drive all such things out of her head.

It was rumoured, Sir Brian at last going away,
Had sent for his charming young hostess to say
All those most correct things a young gentleman
    may,
When some way or other he'd quite lost his head,
And fairly brought out a proposal instead,
While she——well! at least it was plain he had stead,
        And everyone knew,
        And had always known, too,
She was weak in that quarter, and everyone thought
There'd be quite a gay wedding, at least that there
    ought
        To be.   She was so small,
        And he was so tall,
        Such pale Malvoisie,
        Cyprus, sack, eau-de-vie.
None ever had seen, and none ever might see.
        The Ladies Leshakes,
        And Mistress Maude Raikes

Had been asked to be bridesmaids, and everyone
    knew
They would look very charming in silver and blue.
        Then hip! hip! hurrah!
        And huzzah! and huzzah!
Three times three and three more, till we shake the
    old pile,
For Brian, the Knight, and the Lady of Lyle.

PART II.

It is a glorious thing to love,
And own the love for which man strove,
And owning, find how faint and far
E'en fancy's raptured paintings are,
When they would line and form impart
To the weird mine of woman's heart—
To stray at last—knowing and known,
Where never strayed but one alone.
Through all the young life deep and fair,
Through all the dear thoughts guarded there,
Guarded from every other eye,
In girlhood's sweet intricacy.
'Tis thus we see in Eastern tale,
Deep in remote enchanted vale,
Before the destined prince's eyes

The heaven-descended palace rise.
Wondering, he goes from hall to hall,
Some vast, some strange, but glorious all ;
And as he gains the untrodden floor,
Each portal's pictured wealth before,
On the new scene he feasts his eyes,
And lingers o'er the fresh surprise.

And this was Brian's now.   All—all
The guests had fled from that old hall,
And left him with his fair young bride
To feel earth's heaven at her side.
By the clear stream, through the cool grove,
In one long raptured dream they rove,
Heedless of time and all beside,
But that their lives are side by side.
Aylmar's had been the keen pride still
That works itself the most of ill,
Withdrawing, cold, fearful of slight,
Still shaping insult where it might ;
Almost too fearful to offend,
I ween such seldom makes a friend.
But ever to a breast like this,
Is woman's love the truest bliss.
In her deep heart, secure at last,
They pour the longings of the past,
And drink from fount that's never dry

The sweet return of sympathy.
And never on more gentle breast
Did wayward spirit lean to rest,
More skilled in all the arts that bless
The instinct-arts of tenderness,
Than that fair girl's so warm and bright
In her young summer's rosy light,
Whose wealth of joy is with him now,
Of joy—alas! mark that pale brow!

       But first let me say—
       Rather late, by the way—
The poor dear young lady most certainly had
A habit or taste, which at risk I'll call bad,
Or rather, perhaps, to be quite correct, *sad.*
       At three in the day,
       Not once in a way,
But from May to December and then on to May,
A footman brought in on a delicate tray,
The brightest of cups in artistic array,
All filled with the liquid old women called—nay,
They called it no name, but it came from Cathay.
Or the leaves did that made it, with milk 'a votre
    gré,'
Being thought by the young ladies quite a 'succès,'
But voted by men one and all not to pay,
Though they took it of course from the fair Clotilde's
    hands,

And asked for more sugar, and thought of her lands.
For she from the first,
Seemed smit with strange thirst
For the very odd compound, and everyone knew
Who loved the fair heiress must love her tea too.
A line that you see
Just fits.   Ah dear me !
I said it had no name, but then it *was* tea.
And tea, let me tell you, drank often and strong,
Will affect—that's the point--the best nerves before
    long.

It must have been tea,
What else could it be ?
(Besides, Dr. Galen, he said it was tea,
A stout little man with a stout little smile,
Who'd quite a nice practice all around about Lyle).
What else could it be,
That should make young wife see
At twelve every night, by the side of her bed,
A horrible form—with, oh dear ! such a head—
A face of dark blue
Split—yes—quite in two.
With the blood hanging down in black clot from
    each side,
As if it had frozen before it had dried.
And the garments all gory that clung to each limb,

With the ice from each fold standing out like a rim,
In the strange ghastly light that seemed inside
  of him.
      Oh dear! O dear!
      What sights of fear
They must see in the lands that drink tea and not
  beer!

But the lists are set, and the lists are high,
And pennon and streamer merrily
Quiver and curl and dip in the breeze,
As they flutter and flaunt in their degrees;
While lone at one end all may descry,
Sir Brian's blood-red banner fly.
And grimly there his war-horse stands,
Or sniffs the air as it paws the sands,
For the foe that comes not as of old.
And there are his squires, and there unfold
The white wings of pavilion high,
Where stark and stern in his panoply
He has sat since morn and is sitting still,
While the herald has shouted, and shouts with a will,
'Here stands Sir Brian, that very good knight,
Sir Brian de Aylmar, of Lyle, by the right
Of his lady, who sweareth as good knight may,
That if anyone says, or will say or shall say,
That he hath connived at in manner or way,

Or effected or compassed by act, word, or spell,
The death of one Ralf, called Ralf De Lavelle,
He, that said anyone, horribly lies,
As he, the said Brian, most firmly relies,
Will be proved on his body, if here in fair fight
He that lie will maintain, and so heaven help the
   right!'

And there all day in his armour grim,
Plated and mailed, and greave on limb,
Sir Brian sat ready, as good knight can
To prove himself a bloodless man,
And left the lists without speck on his fame,
For he sat there till evening, and nobody came.

       But ah me! ah me!
       And can it be,
In spite of those lists and those words of power,
That very same night in that lady's bower,
In spite of the challenger good and tall,
In spite of the heralds and truncheon and all,
       By the side of her bed
       Stood the thing of dread,
With the very same glare and the very same head,
And the same weak limbs that looked like dead,
And the curdled blood all ice as I said,
And Brian thought that her life had fled.

Ah me ! Ah me !
And so loyally
He had stood against comers great and small —
Yet there—yes there—was the ghost after all !

Yes, there every night,
With its ghastly light,
And the great blue gash that was horrible quite—
That's to say, it was there to that lady's sight,
For nobody else, let them stare as they might,
Could see anything but a curtain white.
It was plainly some freak of her poor dear brain,
But why should that hold such a shape of pain ?
And why should it come again and again ?
And why for the first month that she lay
In her wedded chamber, blithe as may
Could be all her visions ?   Who may tell ?
There must be that hath a deeper spell
Than ever man's mind has yet unravelled—
Immensity where none hath travelled,
Is round and in each soul of ours ;
What sage can fathom his own powers ?
Why should each little lucid ball
Contain the grandest power of all ?
It does not.   We now see through eyes
And think through brains ; but the surprise
In store for each will be to find

Ourselves all sight, that naught can blind
Save our own sin.   Man's one real woe—
Some seem to suffer for other's sin—
But may not each pang a solace win
Of joy eternal ?   Wait for the end—
No pain—no help—no risk—no friend !

And they grew nearer day by day,
As ebbed her fair young life away
Before that nameless horror's sway.
No arm but his her steps might tend,
All other tones her ears offend.
And as she hung upon his breast—
Her one last lingering hope of rest—
She seemed a young vine clinging there,
The closer for the blighting air
That withered, as they outward strove
All tendrils of her life but love.

For all the bright young self is gone.
Thin is her cheek, hollow and wan ;
Vanished the light wit's airy flow,
Her words are feeble, faint and slow ;
For the free step so lithe and strong,
She scarce can drag her limbs along ;
But sadder far than all to see,
Deep gazing into vacancy,

The young eye, large and dark, and clear,
But with its terror ever near,
As though the unutterable dread,
Once all supreme, had never fled
Quite from the portals of the sight.
And yet at times their own old light
Half makes his heaven there again,
Ere comes that weak wild cry of pain,
' O save me, Brian ! save me, save !
Let him not drag me to the grave !

Yes, 'tis a bitter thing to see
The one we love sink wearily,
Like a tired wrestler travel-spent
Into his sleep—but when with rent
Of sudden pain a life is torn,
And death too fearful to be borne
To the young spirit seems, that clings,
To us with all the strength love brings,
Then is the cup o'erturned, I wis—
Pain hath no deadlier pang than this.

PART III.

THE desert wind is drifting dreary
On the fiery Syrian land ;
Parching, withering, restless, weary,
Dying now along the sand ;
Endless, trackless, quivering whitely,
Glares it on the aching sight,
Where with cruel glamour brightly
Jeers the fierce sun in his might.

A ruined column looming vastly
Stands against the distant sky,
Scattered white bones bleaching ghastly,
Mark the traveller's fate more nigh ;
Like some great thought time defying,
Massive, solemn, stern, apart,
Like the withered joys sad-lying
In the desert of man's heart.

Beside the stream the palm-trees grow,
Beside the stream the flowers blow,
Beside the stream from hundred hives,
Glimmer and hum their myriad lives—
If insect life be life indeed,

And not as show of flower and weed
Wee lights and shadows of a whole
To be imprinted on man's soul.
Thither when strays the loitering wind,
Its fiercest breath can softness find,
From rippling bloom and laden spray,
And perfumed green that hides its way
From the unclouded glance of day.
Well might the pilgrim sheltering there
From the white noontide's sultry glare
Dream of his own bright-summer air,
Fresh with the sweep of western main,
Dream that he held that hand again,
Which once to win and hold, I ween,
The sweetness of his life had been.
They stood together, as he thought,
Drinking the sounds the sea-breeze brought
From a far-murmuring strand beneath,
Where still in long and pearly wreath
The tide-swell broke, and further out
With sink and rise, and leap and rout
The tiny wavelets held their way,
Gambolling on that sunny day.
The light fell full on her girlish face,
And something there he thought to trace
Of the dear old pride when her chosen knight
Was conqueror still in mimic fight,

Playing at hide-and-seek with care,
That no other eye should read it there.
But as he gazed came a sadder glow
As on weird and vexèd depths below,
Where hope, and fear, and anguish strove,
And nothing was unmoved but love,
And he knew the look so brightly wan
It bore when first by vow and ban
She knew him a self-banished man
For her dear sake unto the land,
Where once a God's blood dyed the sand—
Perchance to make that look his own,
Angel might stoop from undimmed throne.

But fixèd then her eyes, and lo!
On the horizon's furthest flow
There was a spot that grew and grew
Ever against the westward blue,
Until he marked the billowy sheet,
And low lines of a pinnace fleet,
That seemed to hold in steadfast mood
Its way right on to where they stood;
And soon he felt her closer cling,
As though she feared what it might bring.
Himself could scarcely breathe, he thought,
In mute amaze of wherewith fraught
It came on thus against the land.

No more he heard the murmuring strand,
Nor saw the curling breakers light,
Nor aught except that sail of white :
And still it grew upon the sight,
And still within his breast the thought,
That some mysterious joy it brought,
When ——

       'Palmer, of your courtesy,
I pray you, fair sir, pardon me
That thus must break your reverend dreams—
Such boldness damsel ill beseems.
Yet of your goodness wake, or we
Two here soon dream eternally.'

Beside him bent a dark-browed maid,
One hand upon his shoulder laid ;
The other pointed to the plain
Where turbaned riders spurred amain,
Like hunters who on hard-won day
See a stout quarry brought to bay.
Up sprang the pilgrim at her word,
As one thus waked should grasp a sword,
But sword nor lance were by his side ;
Nor mace nor axe's glistening pride,
Naught but his good staff travel-tryed,
Yet seemed he one from mien and limb

Might take stout foe to cope with him.
Upon the placid streamlet's brink
Two foam-stained horses leaned to drink,
Gaunt were their sides, and gallop-worn,
And one with frequent spurring torn.
But on one saddle drooping fair,
As if fatigue had held her there,
O'ercome with ill and fear of ill;
A Turkish girl sat mute and still;
E'en in that instant's wondering
He thought such face must blessing bring,
Then turned him to the foe again,
And her who pointed o'er the plain.

'Question not yet.   No time to tell—
A convert to the faith.   And well
Our horses served us to this brink,
Now they have fresh ones, and ours sink.'
'Then stand behind me even here
These shrubs will hamper horse and spear,
And there'll be shame on staff and gown,
Or by yon tree the first goes down.'
'The devil may take it from each head,'
So through her teeth the damsel said;
'To try the risk on foot instead—
Just five to two—if things go well
It will be pleasant tale to tell.'

E'en with those words the foe came on
(Yet well he deemed each strangest one
From wandering maiden weak and lone)
With many a shout as prize were won.
Right into the green leaves rode their band,
And stronger growths on either hand;
But scarce was the foremost horseman through,
With head bent low from drooping bough,
When full on his crest a buffet fell
That had stretched, I ween, wild boar as well.
His horse passed on in loose career,
And from baffling sprays the next threw spear
In direst haste to meet such war
With quick grasp of his scimitar.
'Well smote, well smote, thou Palmer bold!
But four are left, and one of them's old.'
Surely a voice of gramarie,
Surely no earthly maiden she
That by his side now took her stand,
With the sabre that dropped from the dead man's
    hand.

'Take that, you rascal, and tell them below
The Christian slave hath mauled you so.'

.   .   .   .   .

The fight is o'er. Upon the plain,
Two Moslem ride with slackened rein —

Two more will ne'er so ride again.
The fifth is senseless on the ground,
And a deep red stain steals his turban round,
And out on the thirsty sand where he lies,
And the chances are all that he too dies.
Then turned the pilgrim to that maid
And wonderingly his eye surveyed
Tall form in Turkish garb arrayed,
The strange smile and the battle blade,
Till with a start, a sudden light
Broke on his yet half-doubting sight.

' Yes, Aylmar, I—hard times have gone
Since last we met—just breath alone
Nor much, was left me at their oar.
If life has one eternal bore,
It's to sit for months chained to a deck,
Rowing all day at some ruffian's beck.
But hard times passed grow fair to view—
Old Sayd may call—ay, marry haloo,
For his slave henceforth, and his daughter too ;
By the way I'll just introduce her to you.'

Bright was the joy of that maiden's eyes,
And bright the laugh of her glad surprise
When they helped her down from her saddle then,
And she saw old friends had met again.

And there by that stream an hour they sat,
There was so much to say about this and that;
And the Palmer shared his simple store,
That in rude wallet still he bore,
And told how, to ease his lady's pain,
He must wander still and wander again,
And ever till a year be done,
Unarmed, unmounted, joyless, lone.
But as the maiden's eye grew dim,
At how pirate horde had seized on him,
Ralf Lavelle grinn'd with many a grin
That soon made little laugh begin—
Yet when the hour had passed, was fain
To ride on with his bride again.

Gone! gone! Alone the pilgrim sate
By the clear stream till it grew late,
And saw his pale face on the wave
So toil-worn grown, and wan and grave,
And thought him of the olden days
When he but lived for deeds and praise,
And dreamed not of the life of care
May lurk behind a face too fair.
Then shuddered at a thought so rude,
So like to base ingratitude—
And saw the sweet face of his dream
Perchance thus sent as comfort's gleam;

And wondered what that thing might be
That in the boat he could not see;
And thought him of his last long kiss,
And almost dared to dream of bliss
That might be in the end—and thought,
Thoughts that that land most near him brought
Of how pain and self sacrifice,
May be of endless love the price;
And how, from hour his vow was made,
Her eye had lost its darker shade,
And wondered was it miracle
Or but the natural joy hearts feel
To know themselves on earth most dear—
A joy may well chase weirdly fear;
And wondered should they meet once more,
And wondering thought it o'er and o'er;
Then laid him down beside the plain,
In hope to dream his dream again.

PART VI.

ALAS! what tales the earth could tell
If clay and sand might speak as well
As drink the life-blood of good men
Or ill, and straight be washed again.
This little stone I throw in air

May once have touched a bosom bare,
That age, and age, and age gone by,
In nature's last extremity,
Crept to its flinty bed to die.
In the fair land where now I write
'Tis told of ancient sainted wight,
' He first held women from the war '
What a strange crimsoned peep afar
Into old depths that line doth give
When she slew by whose pains we live.

On the horizon's far confine,
A broken rise, a curving line,
Mark where an avalanche of sand
O'erwhelmed this morn a pilgrim band.
It came as though the very plain,
Upheaved, had risen and smote and slain.
No shriek of agonising woe,
Rose from the struggling mass below;
The desert waves but closed them o'er,
And settled almost as before,
Save where a solitary tread
Had passed out from among the dead.

And on and on till the fierce rays
Were reddening in one lurid blaze,
Till fire and pain—that almost worst—

The ceaseless agony of thirst,
Might well have made a weaker breast
Long for his comrade's doom and rest;
Might well have crushed him down to lie
Upon the burning plain and die.
But Brian quailed not first or last,
Though the fell simoon's rushing blast,
The fall, the eager strife with death,
The upward heaving into breath;
Nay, when alone above the sand
He could not grasp one living hand,
But rising passed over their tomb
To meet his solitary doom,
In fire and toil and lingering pain,
Of thirst upon the desert plain,
He never quailed, but with a prayer
That was too faithful for despair,
And one deep loving thought ' for thee,'
Strode on into the desert sea.

And now, as in a lurid dream,
All things unreal and clouding seem;
Strange voices murmur through his brain,
Strange lustres glimmer o'er the plain.
When sudden on his startled ear—
Above, behind, below, but clear—
A sound of music in the air

Breaks wondrously—no note of care,
No wild harsh breathing of despair;
But fast and light, a merry air,
Yet with a ghastly merriment,
As though to speed the dance 'twere meant,
That fair Lucerne's bridge beneath
Gives a grim pleasantry to death.
'Twas strange how that weird jocund strain,
Smote with a keen resistless pain,
Into his soul—as we in dream
To feel a coming horror seem—
Ere yet he knew, but knew too well,
Those notes, that air—'twas thine, Lavelle!

Alas! the sun above is fire,
A red sun blasting in its ire,
And the white plain is fire below,
But cold as winter's ice-breath now,
The shivering life-blood curdling pressed
Back upon Aylmar's labouring breast.
A sudden dread palsied his brain—
Had all his toil and care been vain?
Had he made false his solemn vow?
Nor arms nor steed might it allow,
Yet by his staff two foemen slain,
Looked up to Heaven from battle-plain—
If they *were* men—and not a show

Of demons sent to tempt him so—
Perchance he pressed no mortal hand,
Nor convert saved from Moslem band,
But was in all things sport of foes
The deadliest that our nature knows.
Yet had he willed to do no wrong,
And *will* God judges—from his vest
That deeply folded o'er his breast
A cross such as in Syrian land
The pilgrims bear, rose in his hand.
'Back, fiend!' he said, and firmer trod,
'Leave thou the sinner to his God!'
Was it a shriek that passed him there,
A vague weak wailing of despair—
So full of hate and yet of pain?—
At least those notes came not again.

But on again, with steadier stride,
As though that victory supplied
Fresh strength to failing limb and breath,
Fresh vigour for the strife with death
He strode—until the maddening thirst
Upon him agonizing burst,
And over every power of thought
One fierce resistless longing brought
A longing to lie by the brink
Of a cool endless stream and drink.

And lo! before him, glistening bright
In the weird sunshine's dreamy light,
Was water!—water!—a broad tide,
Wooing his faint steps to its side.

Alas! at other hours, full well
He would have known that lying spell;
Have known, have marvelled, and passed by;
But now, in Nature's agony,
Half overthrown is reason's sway,
And instinct has its grosser way.
Still doubting half, and half in fear
He drags his limbs—just fainting—near,
Near, till he sees his lengthening shade
Upon the seeming water made.
Why starts he so? Lo! by that brink
No stooping Palmer leans to drink;
But turban'd face, so fierce, so fell,
Well might he deem that it was Hell
That darkened in its lurid glare,
That laughed through all the mocking air,
As swept that lying vision past—
Nature's last strength is spent at last.
With cross grasped in his rigid hand,
Brian lies senseless on the sand.

'Rest! pilgrim, rest! thy task is done,

Thy sins are cancelled, the goal is won ;
The power of the fiend of thy life is o'er,
And joy will be thine for evermore ;
The prayer of the woman that loves thee well
Hath guarded thy steps through each perilous spell.'
Was it a dream that o'er him past ?
Do dying men dream thus at last ?
Those stooping forms that round him glide,
The camel looming by his side,
The whispered comfort in his ear,
The gentle face so very near,
Now fading into dream.   If this
Be death, life hath scarce dearer bliss !

Within the convent's lofty wall,
Beneath the convent's turret tall,
Where almost fortress-like they rose,
With rest for friends and frowns for foes ;
Where the wide trees made pleasant shade,
A Palmer's languid form is laid.
Gaunt is his frame and sickness-worn,
His rugged garb is stained and torn,
Yet well those sordid weeds below
The eye a warrior's form may know.
And even now, though scarce its length,
His frame in slow returning strength
Could drag to that soft summer shade,

Where evening winds a coolness made,
There's something in his eager look,
That tells of soul that scarce can brook
The weakness it may not defy—
That soft enervate luxury
Which fever leaves so oft behind,
With men of strongest mould and mind.
' Father, ere yet to-morrow's sun
Look on my homeward path begun,
A path that scarce will cheer the less,
Though steps may falter while they bless;
(For now, with evening's hour draws near,
The ending of my exile year—
Yes! even while yon shadow falls—)
Ere yet I leave these gentle walls
I still would crave one favour more,
His name who brought unto your door
This fevered dying senseless frame—
Well may I long to know that name!'

' You will not give it? I can see
Denial in averted eye.
Then I must, blundering on, *all* love,
Lest I to one ungrateful prove;
But now another favour still—
This you must grant me—nay, you will
There's one in yonder guarded cell

To whom I'd gladly say farewell
Ere yet I part.   A novice young,
Perchance.   For me the strains she sung
Soothed many an hour of restless woe,
As fever-chained I tossed below.
Oh! many a weary night of pain
I've longed to hear that voice again ;
Longed for the gentle hymn that stole
Like Heaven's own comfort on my soul ;
Or the sweet melody of earth,
That seemed scarce less of holy birth,
So full of peace and joy and rest,
And grateful happiness, it blessed.
And, father, often it would seem —
So sick men no doubt ever dream—
As though it eased some secret pain
Of my own heart.   But hark! again!'

Song (*from the window above*).

Come back! come back!
Over the patient sea
Where the waves roll ceaselessly,
Rising and falling before my sight,
From weary morn till weary night—
        Come back!

I've counted all the hours away,
My life's been counting to this day,
And it was near, and it has come
Upon an empty empty home—
        Come back!

Love! were a thousand folds of sea
Between this fated eve and me,
A thousand seas should conquered be;
Unharm'd I'd pass their desert sands,
Unharm'd through all their burning lands,
      To thee!

Fool! now struck down by toil or war,
Perchance thy hero lies afar;
Perchance, through nights of fire and pain,
He calls, alas! and calls in vain,
      On thee!

No, he is near, he hears. Ere long
He'll know who sings this simple song;
I'll hear his step, I'll see his face,
My head will find its own old place—
      My love, my love!

I'll tell him how, on desert lone,
The hand that soothed him was his own;
Who it was here from casement dim
That still could sing and pray for him.
I'll tell him all, when on my brow
I feel his kiss—his kiss—now, now—
      My love, my love!

The tale is told.   For many a year
That ancient convent hoar and drear
A very fairy-house, in dream,
To two, beside the waste, did seem;
And oft, with tiny gibe or praise,
Wee baby mouths babbled of days

Mamma hunted papa of old
And found him on a Syrian wold.

And now, if anyone shall ask
What is the drift of this my task,
And do I think such had not been
If no vow had been vowed—I ween
I shall not answer yea or nay.
I've told my tale, and go my way.

RICHARD GREVILLE.

—--◦◦•—--

By the gate they stood.
'It cannot be,' he said; 'I felt before
Water and words make not such severance.
At two o'clock the child were lost for ever,
By three the priest has come and done his office,
And, lo! it is a little saint to pray to!
Yet God is just, and justly still rewards
And punishes.   How can all these things be?'

Her face was very white, and on her lip
A tremble rippled faintly as she answered:

'It seems to me in such a world as ours,
Where all is mystery—our own poor selves
A mystery to ourselves—sight, hearing, thought,
The very movement of obedient limbs,
All mysteries—the less we dream of things
That are beyond the fathoming of our minds

The better. God hath willed that we submit
Those minds to Him ; it is our offering.'

' That is the cant—submit, submit,' he grumbled.
' Can you not see I fear to do the will
Of men and not my Maker's, thus submitting
Against the warning of the mind He gave ?
Hear the one answer I could see to this—
Duty of mind begins at home and ends ;
Each mind can rule one path, the rest is God's,
Who hath a myriad ways of being just
We may not reckon of.   It is His choice
To give to outward signs a power for us
Whose wills observe or not observe.   For *us*, then,
For *us* they are most real.   " Ask ye him,"
So was it said of old, " who meeteth you
With pitcher on his head, and he will shew
The room where we may eat the pasch together."
Well might the wondering brethren answer, "Master,
Since Thou canst make him meet us on the way,
Surely he can prepare without our bidding."
Yet was their journey the act requisite
Not for that other's virtue, but for theirs.
So could God save the child without the water,
But we neglecting it shall not be saved.'

The moon seemed brighter on her face. 'The thought,
The very thought,' she said, ' I longed to speak.'

Then mark here how it turns against yourself.
The mind was given to each to guide one path
By such truth it may feel or grasp or touch.
This is our axiom.   Well, apply it boldly.
The faith's unchangeable being once revealed,
Once and for ever, to the chosen twelve,
Therefore the fathers held the Pope infallible,
And yet so holding judged him heretic,
Drawing no nice distinction in the matter.
There is no mystery here; all facts, plain facts,
And thus within the scope of our mind's action.
If they had heard of our fine shadowings,
Think you they had not marked them then?
Think you, if now a Pope were dealt with in this
    fashion,
Such lines were not the foremost marks of all,
Lest scandal should descend to doubting men?
And why not then, if they believed as now?'

'They then believed,' she said, 'but in the Church,
Therefore no scandal came of such their act.
Now we believe the pope is chosen by God
To be the Church's mouthpiece through the years.
The voice is still the same, the Church's voice,
Though coming from the lips of Peter only.'

'Why should they make such radical change so late?'

He said, and saying crushed a gritty morsel
Of lime from the stone piers between his fingers.
'I'll tell you why.   They reasoned thus, Catherine.
To meet societies of secret men
On equal ground, we must have discipline
As strong as theirs.   The Pope's our grand master,
And he must rule by hell as theirs by daggers.
That is the main point—discipline, discipline—
Your metaphysics are at best but cloudland.
Grant that we weaken our position there,
We'll strengthen it on ground compact and real.
Let liberal zealots prate.   We have the peasants
Who vote and fight—good honest souls, who care not
For history or arguments, or such stuff.
As for the others, let them yield or go.
Better have ninety drilled than the full hundred
With two strong wills on most material points.
Such was their reasoning; mind you, it implied
Some thought like this at bottom: 'Yes, heaven's
     good,
If there be heaven.   Meanwhile our Rome is
Without an "if" at all.'

                              'Oh, how unjust,'
She answered, and then paused. 'From you, too; you
Who lay such stress on truth, so loving it.
Surely if it be *true* the Pope errs not,

Defining certain doctrines from his chair,
And so the Church believes, she should proclaim
The fact, and take no benefit from clouds
Wrapping her truth round as some fabled mist
Of old protected fainting hero's life.
The Church faints not, but ever dares the combat.'

'*If* it be true?' he said. 'O what a word
Is "if." Alas! it is not true, Catherine.'
'And yet I've heard you say a thousand times
Who will believe in one must still grant all.
If Christ was God, then is the Church His Church.'

'Have said and say. I have no option—none.'

'And can you, will you, part with all?—with all?
No hope, no trust in God; no faith, no Christ?
For God's sake, Richard, not for mine, repent.
I do not mean repent—I scarce know what
I mean. Yield not your faith. Oh think of life
And all its woes, its terrible woes, Richard.
Ere long you will be sick and die; die hopeless,
In pain, in agony, without a hope.
What that must be!'

     The light was on her face,
The pale light glaring through the slender trees

Upon her hood and careless mantle's fold,
And all the eager pleading of her eyes,
And o'er his inmost soul a longing came
To take her to his heart and whisper 'You
Shall be my faith—you only—you for ever.'
But he moved not, and said, 'And think you, Catherine,
I need that baser thought to make me long
For power to feel as you?   All my best hopes,
Best thoughts, best dreamings from my mother's
    knees,
Have clung to that that they have now wrenched
    from me.
For years my waking lips will form a prayer
Instinctive to the—— but it matters not.
Why harrow you with thoughts like these? I believe
Still in the Maker who hath made you, Catherine,
And in His truth and justice.   So we part.'

'Then you must go, Richard?'

                        'Yes, I must go.
More days than I could spare I've given already
To this and the old times from yonder city.
I'll write always to Bella.   Need I say,
One word, and I am back—by telegraph!'

He smiled, and, with a long grasp of the hand,

Was on the road to Dijon.   Then she gathered
Her slender cloak around her, and walked back
Along the straight drive to the ancient house.
Half way there was an iron seat for two,
And scarcely knowing what she did, she sat;
It was so dark there, the wide sycamore
Rising beyond, and no one near, she felt,
To hear her long low wail, or see her slight form
Shake with its agony of tears.   Yet soon
There was a step, and on a breast she lay,
And sweet warm lips, sweet as her own, I think,
Purred over her a gentle loving purr
Till she grew calm again.   'So he has gone,'
They said at last, 'gone, and has left you thus.
If I were he, before—now God forgive me—
I think I'd be Mahometan or-- Turko,
Dyed a sweet shade of polished dinner-table;
I'm sure I'd look quite faithful.   Let me laugh!
You know it all will come right in the end.
Two people that are fond as you and he
Don't quarrel for their lives about the Pope,
Dear good old man—I wish I was the Pope,
To ban the fellow now with book and candle.'

'Hush, Bella! 'tis my doing; mine, God help me!
He cannot think but what he thinks.   Nor would I,
For my poor sake, he falsified his thought.'

'Confirming, pet, a little view that struck me
Quite forcibly to-day watching you two.
We've left the world, I mean *that* world, this long
    time,
And now torment each other in the next.
Nobody goes to heaven straight, you know,
But dead still think they live, mounting by inches.
I died—well now, I'm not quite sure—but think
We all died in the lake last year at Vevey.
Yes, that was it; the storm upset us then—
Our boat as well as stomachs—and were drowned.
A charming fancy, worthy Richard's self;
Who, all his fine talk notwithstanding, dear,
Is superstitious quite beyond your dreaming.
You think its from high virtue he won't take
His faith for granted, like the rest of us.
Not so : but just that he may paint his pictures.
His pencil won't go straight, nor thoughts come right,
If false to what he calls his better self.
His worse, we know it ; proper papists ready
To roast six heretics if they would let us—
That is the wretch's miserable secret—
Don't say I " peached," or he will ne'er forgive me.'

' I will not " peach," yet think you wrong him there,
    too.
He holds his art to be a high vocation

Direct from heaven, as such still to be served
With all but sin.   It is a noble faith.'

'And yet so thinking you have cast him from you—
In purgatory most decidedly.
Now there's the very look poor Richard painted
In sweet Saint Somebody, that spat her tongue out
At Roman Consul, Prætor, or such person.
I knew I'd somewhere seen a live one like it ;
There was a glare of torches on the face, though,
And not the moon—pale moon—how fast it rises.
I did not mean to put you on the rack, dear,
But take it, it's the custom of the place
To bother most where we would try to comfort.'

'My own, if this is purgatory, then
Are you the angel sent to be its solace ?'

'There's really much in favour of the view,
Not of that last, you know, but as a whole,'
Laughed Bella then. 'I wish, as Richard says,
You'd bring a philosophic spirit to it ;
But now come in, for I have got the keys.'

And they both rose and up the walk moved slowly
To the broad sand before the ancient house,
And so into the study of its master—

Ancient almost as it—their grandfather ;
Half Irish, who, in times nearly forgotten,
Drew maiden sword for France and Emperor.
Before him sat the village curé then,
With journal on his knee, and both were loud
With patriotic ardour and for Church.
Wrapped in those brown-black lines lay the great
    news,
War ! war !—the Emperor had declared it—war !
The troops were flooding all the roads since morning :
Zouaves, Line, Imperial Guards, guns, chasseurs,
    Turcos.
The Prussians would be nowhere, that but followed.
Who can withstand French soldiers in fair battle ?
Fools ! fools !—God can !

               But Greville took the train
Next morn for Switzerland, and wandered long
By her blue lakes and breezy mountain paths,
Catching the far-off echoes as he rose
Of tramp of nations hurrying beneath.
But not for him was worship of great sights,
To some almost as worship of their God.
What were the mountains after all but stones,
Great knotted shoulders of the skeleton earth,
That sweeps clay-covered on its path for ever
Through masses larger than itself ?   Useless

Were there no minds to scan them in their course,
As would be brightest dyes if light were not.
'Tis we that make the Alps great in whose souls
They wake great thoughts, or bright imaginings,
Fulfilling His designs whose dust they are.
So Richard deemed, but had no bright thoughts
    then,
Nothing but fretful yearnings and vague sense
Of all things being disjoint and purposeless,
And love being very dear, yet dearest love
A mockery if it ends with death.   And hate,
Plenty of hate, he had for that which wrenched
His peace away from him and promised wife.
And hating still, half-craved for German gain
In battle—longing that the right should win
Lest Ultramontane truths be true enough—
Yet thinking, too, of claims blood-near and love,
Old love of artist, warrior, thinker, saint,
In that fair southward land somewhat his own.
But his was not the France that thronged below
With rifles tried at Mentana, and grape-guns
Not tried as yet—Voltaire, or worse at heart,
Holding high sway at Rome—rather the France
That, half-armed, flung all Europe from her bounds
As from a crater rent with passionate right
In old volcanic times; or yet that other
That daily sends out pale and resolute men

To die for Christ ; or best, his dream of France
Who would have joined two noblest faiths in one,
The monk loving the young that the young loved.
She would not follow him or his, therefore
The painter loved her not, loved her not then ;
Rather those Germans who had bishops bishops,
(For most that keen sore rankled) and homes, homes,
And thought all men should stand upon their side ;
And almost cursed his country that she sat still
Turning her wretched pennies, nor as once
Sprang up in arms with clang that nations shook ;
Yet trusted much in right and German men,
And almost lovingly looked northward—he,
Republican and Catholic—once Catholic.
So varying are the thoughts of varying minds,
Yet not inconsequent, perchance, in this.

And soon he scarce could drag his listless steps
Far from the centres of congested thought,
Knowing each hour might bring strange news.   Yet
    once
Climbing a steep at early morn, by noon
Had looked from green slope opening among pines
Down on a valley where a swift stream wound
Glittering the while through lazy village smoke,
With steep hills on the other side, and upward
A far white dome against the cloudless sky.

And, choosing spot amid the outer trees,
Where checkered light played on the yellow moss,
He stretched himself and gazed, but tried no sketch,
And slowly slept at last.
                        When he awoke
Another stood, where he had stood at first,
Gazing as he gazed ; one that he had seen
The night before at his hotel and marked,
Yet scarce had deemed him so well worthy mark
As now, when in his solitary stand
(Then but a gentle-looking man in black),
Soul shining out responsive, Richard thought,
He well were model of some chaste contemplative
To whose calm feet the hunted deer would steal
In olden forest brake, secure of life.
And when the stranger's hand made a quick sign,
Deeming himself alone, the painter knew
There was short prayer for so much beauty given,
And straight in heart went out unto him then,
Yet lay unmoved and would have feigned to sleep
Had he been seen, fearing a spy might grieve ;
But when the other went upon his way
Followed, and when ere long cross-ways were passed,
Joined on and spoke to him, and so together
Returned, already friends—hard-working priest
Whose health had failed him, and now drank it
    there

In lungfuls of pure mountain air—English,
Who had before his turn of doing Paul Pry,
Seeing the artist, tall impulsive Greville,
Refuse old woman alms, sadly refuse,
And rush on fumbling at his pocket, then,
As if he found small coin in damaged corner,
Turn and rush back, and leave at last well-blessed,
Seen from the window all the while.   So the two
Were friends that day, and comrades for a week,
Looking at mountains and not often silent.
Old schoolfellows beside, though scarce remembered,
For Edmund Vaughan was monitor and what not
When Richard took his first nine ferulas—
Proud, the young rascal, that he had not flinched—
And gently, as he found his friend could bear it,
Fearing each word might numb like those old strokes,
The painter poured out all his soul at last—
For still the other tried to coax him on,
Knowing who'd heal a wound must probe it first,
And honest reasoning the lance of truth.
' All Atheists in fact, though not in thought,
It may be ; else they had not done it then.
The very worst of godlessness is lying
To serve what we call truth, and wrong inflicting
In the sweet name of justice.   They have lied
Now a great public open palpable lie,
Having still loved to lie, as he wrote once,

The good man who went down into his grave
With agony of warning on his lips,
Happy he might not live to see the end.'
So Richard said, gnawing grass-stalk the while.
And then again, ' As for injustice, look you,
What can be more unjust than this Rome business ?
Here are we Liberals, we Irish such,
Whose primal doctrine is that States are free
To choose their rulers, shrieking with one voice
(A rather cracked one, with good Adrian
And Ireland handed over in the mind)
That Rome shall not be free, but be our Popes.
'Tis our *religion* that it be our Popes,
His Vicar, who hath said, Not of the earth
My kingdom.   Surely if it be of God,
The Pope should reign in Rome, he will reign there
Without *wrong* done by you.   Rome is not yours ;
Give Dublin, if you will, Paris or Brussels
Or see that Roman votes are free—that's fair,
That only.   Then there comes that worst of all,[1]
The clinging to old horrors as to right,
Because so held in fierce crime-darkened days ;
Aye, even justifying the sin of sins,
When human souls were scorched out for their
  · thoughts,
Or made deny those thoughts by agony.

[1] See Appendix, note A.

Just fancy if some pleasant Torquemada,
Or for that matter pleasant Council of Constance,
Could catch me here with their sweet 'Sign or burn!'
What wonder if free minds hold Voltaire saint
Rather than Veuillot —— ?'

                                   'Hold neither saint,'
Said Father Vaughan, smiling, 'so that's ended.
These then, it seems, are your three difficulties—
That certain persons in the Church approve
Of burnings, Inquisitions, and the rest;
That certain other persons, Liberals,
Will speak of Roman things illiberally;
And third, the definition pure and simple,
Clear proof of all of us being Atheists.
Now on the first head I will only say
(Not having thought much of such things—so busy—
Much hoping, too, the Pope shall have again,
I will not say his own, but that his own
Will have him—kind old man, that loves the poor)
My own opinions coincide with yours,
Or nearly so I deem, yet never give me
One passing thought of personal discomfort.
Until we're told by holy Church herself
We are no sons of hers holding these thoughts,
Let idle talkers talk. If they can't see
What we see, let us go our way unminding
And pray for them, yet not forget ourselves—

Never forget ourselves.

     The third remains.

And first I'll tell you that my own good bishop,
A man whose thoughts were heaven and duty, died
While they debated, and died all conjuring
To crown the Church this-wise. Yet for myself
What little I could do I did, but little,
To have the matter left as it had stood,
And even now think our position weakened
By this decree as a converting Church.[1]
But as to doubt, I never thought of it;
Just as I would not doubt should some strong sophist
Show reason for belief I had no hand;
Or if a stranger called my brother thief
For specious cause assigned that puzzled me.
I might not answer these particular arguments,
But feel I have my hand, and there's an end.
So with the faith. I know that Christ is God,
The Church His Church. The reasons I can bring
In favour of my faith are stronger far
Than those against, yet scarce through these I know,
But rather through a trust free-given by God.'

' Then if the Church is weakened,' Greville said,
' It could not be God's will that definition.'

     [1] See Appendix, note B.

'Why not? The faith contained before hard things,
And now contains one more. All might be easy
If God so willed, but such is not His will.
Rather it is His will, it may be, you
And such as you should honour Him and truth
Fighting with doubts, yet seeking still that Will—
For you I hold never quite Catholic.

Listen—this is the reasoning, I think.
We men must have a Maker, else the queen-bee
And Plato are facts unaccountable.
But having Maker, we should honour Him,
Or minds were made for nothing. Christ is He.
Now dwell on that, and go no further, Greville,
Not till you've prayed a month. Forget the Pope,
Saints, Congregations, Fathers, Councils, Church.
You feel there is a God. Then ask yourself,
Is not Christ He? and pray to God to know;
Remembering, if not God, He was Impostor.

'The thought, the very thought,' the painter muttered,
She gave—"I cannot be your wife so holding."

'And thank God, Richard, for that lady's love.
Yes, you have much to thank for, Richard—much.
Pray; that's the main point, pray; and write to me
After one month. You know the place; good-bye.'

And so they parted, and still Greville went
Thinking among the hills—thinking for ever.

But she—she who had loved him since the two
Shared the one garden, leaving Bella's single,
When first the little Irish pair came orphans—
Bella the cousin, Richard her half-brother—
Owning thenceforth his schoolboy's confidence,
Not given in the short and ill-spelt notes,
But words vacation-spoken in those rambles
Through the sweet lanes and grapes just ripening;
When Bella often stayed with grandpapa,
Filling his pipe and reading in the shade,
Taking him all herself when Richard came,
The confidence of proud and nervous boy—
Quick at his books, and games, and grief, and
    dream—
Boy elbowing his steadfast upward way
To be best runner, Grecian, cricketer.
Then leaning on his opening thoughts of things
And loving his new power as artist—catching
The fragrance of old walks in many a view;
But above all, sharing, as I said, thoughts—
Given by letter these times—letters kept
Inviolate in inmost shrine of shrines,
Much to be quizzed but never seen by Bella,
(Who sometimes wrote herself—saddest of times)

Until all knew—or grandpapa and Bella knew—
That Richard made a hundred pounds in six months,
And ere the next new year the two should marry.
But she

      Smiled still—pale smile—and went her way
To the church mostly ; and let Bella kiss her,
And read the newspapers aloud all day,
As in a dream—a dream of guns and men—
And felt that she and youth were parted wholly,
Yet had no peace—no peace—not even in prayer;
That now was driest duty—duty still,
Though some dull instinct fought against it ever,
As part of that which thus had robbed her life
Of all its joy, and other life than hers,
Perhaps for nothing—it might be for nothing.
Often before had she refused his thoughts,
Yet ever found them golden in the end,
The brighter for the struggle, so perchance—
But then a sudden start would check her. 'Hold!
Will you, then, doubt the God who died for you?'
And quick as thought her slender hand would press
A little cross that lay within her breast;
Press from outside, so nobody could mark,
But found no comfort in it—peace nor comfort;
Nothing but duty.
        And meanwhile there came

The great news Richard longed for on his hills,
The Prussians had been somewhere—everywhere—
A French head nowhere. Courage, fighting, plenty;
But wisdom all gone off to Moltke and Bismark.
Minerva with the Greeks, and no sun-god
For the poor Trojan side. Right had its fill.
But little reading now, and soon the girls
Knew that the fine old face was strangely older—
Haggard almost. Marked, too, the sword was stirred,
The old sword hanging between dusty pistols
Beside the bed; sword that had seen Moskowa,
And now was drawn to give back ancient face,
It might be, looking on it. Who could tell?
Perhaps the wind had moved it, or a shock
Of sudden-closing door, and not the hand
Of palsied old man thinking oft of him
Whose form, grey-coated, shone upon the wall.

But Catherine ever prayed her dreary prayer,
Till one day, when the vesper chaunt arose
In the old parish church—she kneeling, darkly,
Bent o'er her chair before the Virgin's altar,
Where the stained light from cobweb'd saints above
Just tinged the shadowy floor—as that long loved,
The hymn that heralds benediction's rite,
Swept through the aisles, and one clear plaintive
    voice,

That seemed to rise as her own soul would rise,
With all its weight of anguish to the Lord's feet
To lay it there, thrilled out the last glad words,
The whole joy of the song burst in upon her.
'To us, to us ; yes, Lord, us *both*,' she breathed,
'In our own fatherland.'   And lo, there seemed
An answer in her heart.   'My faithful one,
Blessed are they that mourn as thou hast mourned.'
And fast and hot a blinding rain of sweetness
Burst through her quivering lids and close-pressed
    fingers.
It was so long since she had had a joy.

On that same day this letter went to London.

' I quite grant Deism has one great want,
Hinting at no self-sacrifice in God,
Self sacrifice of virtues the most godlike,
Who to be God must be all virtue's essence ;
No fellowship in pain with world of pain,
And therefore love the Christian thought of Him.
Deem, too, the evidence historical,
Of that thought's truth most wonderful if false,
Still have my one great stumbling-block unmoved,
Knowing if Christ was God, your church was His,
And she has lied.   I know your Church was His,
For what we call the Faith is but God's picture,

His sacred likeness left to human souls,
To make them happier, as He left at first
Some shadow of His beauty on the hills,
And to be picture real it must be *one*,
Not confused blending of *discordant* sketches.
God had not died to leave such mist to man,
But rather gave His likeness to His Church—
If Christ was God—with trust that she should guard
Each sacred line with her whole life of lives.
To take an instance from the best of sects :
The Lord is with us in a sacrament,
Bodily present, as He was on earth,
So says the Catholic Church. What says the English?
Just nothing, for part says this too, or nearly,
While other part calls out ' Idolatry ! '
Now what strange rendering of the gift divine ;
If true, whole revelation of His goodness.
Both views give blended, yet both views are hers.
God had not died to leave such mist to man.

' Here you will hold with me, but I write thus
To prove you cannot sever Christ from Church
As you would have me, or at least that I can't.
If Christ was God, then is the Church His Church,
And surely Pope and Council were the Church ;
And they have lied, so there's an end of all——
An end of all.

' Perhaps it might be said
The Pope errs not when he *defines* a doctrine
Of faith and morals to the listening world
(For Christian morals are the path to God
Through human happiness, and perfect life
Some faint and far-off shadow of the Lord [1]).
And this being so, Honorius then *defined* not,
But merely *put an end* to controversy,
Helping wrong side. But, mark you, Ultramontanes
Will pull away that plank, deciding sternly
The word " define " in no way means *define*,
But means—mark you, it means—*finem imponere*,
The very thing Honorius did.

       I doubt
If Luther, Calvin, Voltaire, all alive,
Could pull down better than your Ultramontanes
For their view's sake.'

     Ere two weeks more were gone,
A letter came, bearing the Zurich post-mark,
To grandpapa, that in a stranger's hand
Gave worst of news in terms cold and fretful.
' A Mr. Richard Greville had a fever
In their hotel.'   He, the proprietor,
Held sharpest hopes some one would come to tend
 him,

---

[1] Of course not in the same sense as dogmas of the faith.

Having already had much losses in the matter.
Scarce was the letter read when trunks were packed,
And by midday both girls, seated in train,
Annette, sage bonne, being left with grandpapa.
They stood at night—the two—by Richard's bed-
side,
Who knew them not; therefore had Catherine ven-
tured.
His brain was much engaged—that is the term,
I think—his fancies of the queerest.   Strong still
In voice and limb, but brain engaged enough.
Poor Bella sat ever listening to all.
But from that night he mended, and soon lay
In almost endless sleep, waking himself,
Or near himself.   Sure to get well, all said;
The joy that they were with him the best tonic.
And soon again came sittings up in state,
With Catherine welcomed in as visitor;
Sweet cheery evenings by the open window,
With breezes from the lake, gentlest of breezes;
Theology forbidden by nurse Bella.
Yet soon that, too, was past, and it was queen
Of morning strolls and saunterings in boat.
His life was ruined—that was still his moan;
Life that before had been so straight and bright,—
A ladder tending to a definite end,
'With room for two on each rung, Catherine.'

The only rational aim of rational man
Was in all things to do his Maker's bidding,
So seeking ever for his brother's good,
In each act 'greatest good of greatest number ; '
That Maker who, as Christians taught, could create
A universe at wish, but to make saint,
A free will that obeyed, did die in torture.
But now all this was past.   Yet Longfellow
Had said, ' If Christian faith gave nothing better
Than Mary to the world, it was the best
The world had seen.   And he would work again,
He thought, upon his picture—Mother looking
Upon her Infant's hands.   If nothing more,
The Christian dream had surely been man's noblest,
And that was much.

                    Just then, the two slow-strolling
Along the shaded street, passed a small church.
' Come in and rest one moment,' Catherine said.
And they went in and heard a preacher preaching
In French, a stranger to some strangers there,
On Pope Infallible, and so they listened.
But ere the sermon ended, Richard whispered
' Come home, come home; there's something I would
     see,'
And walked so fast outside she scarce could follow,
The perspiration on his face the while.

'A thought—I've got a thought,' he said, 'most
   curious,
And want to see a Testament at once ;
Come on ! come on !' And she went on, now praying,
And heard ere long his quick step up the stairs,
And stood by Bella writing, but still thought
'What can it be ? What can it be so moved him ?'
Till he came down again, the book in hand.
'I see it all,' he said ; 'I see it all.
I never thought the " you " was plural, never ;
Which makes the whole thing plain. The Lord was
   giving,
On the great night of all, his last instructions :
"Satan hath longed,"—these are the words,—" to
   sift you,"
(That's scatter you in fifty thousand sects,
As wheat is scattered through dividing sieve)
" But I have prayed for thee, thee Peter Pope,
That thy faith fail not, and that thou converted
Confirm the brethren "—that is make them steadfast,
Being the bond of union that prevents
Such scattering of the Church. Could words be
   plainer ?' [1]

' Which means I'll buy a certain ring to-morrow,'
Said Bella, rising and demurely curtseying.

[1] See Appendix, note C.

'Children, receive my most sincere condolence,
Or benediction, if you like it better ;
But as I have to write to grandpapa,
And Catherine has her things on, pray go out
And talk the matter over by the lake.'

Talk thought of long.   Meanwhile the rumour
    grew
Of Prussian advent, darkening the old house
Amid its straight trim trees—old house seigniorial,
Where sons had died for France age after age,
Now held by ancient officer half Irish—
Rumour too soon of fact.   Dijon was taken,
And Bella's brown mare requisitioned ; bay, too,
Though for the moment left in their old quarters.
A Captain Somebody, and Lieutenant Von ——,
The names don't matter much—took the best bed-
    rooms,
The best of everything ; giving for thanks
Much German rendering of 'thunder and turf,'
As white-haired Larry put it, Bella's groom,
Now general factotum, curious in French,
Whose face at requisitions was a marvel ;
Yet comforted by thinking of the 'boys,'
And what short work they'd make of them same
    'Prooshians.'
Glad, too, the poor old master was in bed,

Or there'd be murder done some day, 'for sartin.'
Good honest Larry, tending the old man,
Who from that bed heard Teuton melodies,
Warmed by his wine. Old man nigh brokenhearted,
Oft looking to his sword and Emperor,
And better things than these—good, brave old man—
Until at last the strain became too great,
And by his ordering they wrote to Greville

Letter which missed—-for he that night reached
   Dijon,
No longer German in good will, far from it;
Admiring much their burly regiments,
But with his heart all given to France again.
Poor France, that strove so nobly in defeat—
The France that yet might lead the world to right,
Thus purified at home and just to all.
He passed some Uhlans ere he reached, walking,
The gate where he and Catherine parted last.
Fires had been lighted on the trodden grass,
And German voices echoed from the windows.
But heeding not, he passed in through the porch
And found all gathered in his own old room—
Annette and Larry, and the grandpapa—
His own old room, but on the wall the sword
And pistols and the Emperor. There, too,
A copy of the Scheffer he had painted

And given long ago—a face he loved.
The old man's was much changed, yet brightened
   fast
Then as they spoke.   Glad, too, that he had come
Before the letter reached.   He must leave that—
These Germans were fast killing him—but how?
Then Larry interposed, his keen grey eyes
Just peering in their fun.   Miss Bella's mare
And the old bay were in the stable still,
And the light britska.   'Sure he'd harness them
Just quiet-like, afore the gintlemin
Beyant had done their punch, and slip out back-
   wards,
That's if their honours liked, to-night.   He knew
A way that stole over the hills in no time ;
Maybe they'd never miss the bastes till morning.'
It was a pleasant plan, and so accepted,
The old man growing ten years younger straightway,
And Annette smuggling in a dinner, both
Kept very quiet till the punch hour came,
And with it shadows darkening through the trees.
Then, wrapped in ancient cloak, the veteran—
The pistols by his side and sword once more—
Leaning on Richard's arm, mounted the carriage ;
And they drove gently out upon the grass.
The brown mare's neck arched double, and the bay
Old horse but sure, as good at need or better,

And Larry bending over reins, a picture.
' The silver tight under the sate yer honours ? '
A gate opened by Richard brought them straight
On rough clay track amid close-cultured fields,
That tried the springs a little, but they failed not.
And so on to a road, then off again,
By old half-grass-grown wind, the brown mare
   bounding,
And grandpapa almost as young as Richard,
Drinking the free night air fast blowing round them.
Up hill and down, then out, and slow ascent—
But not a Uhlan seen—an hour's ascent.
Then as the road swept under darkening pines,
A narrow road, with on the other side
The brawl of streamlet many a yard below,
Old Larry gathered up his reins, the incline
Beginning downward, and the still fresh horses
Were answering gaily to the call, when Richard
Stood up and listened.   ' Hold, hold, Larry, hold !
Hold man, I say ; listen, I think I hear
The sound of horses on the road behind.'
' Myself is bothered Master Richard, dear,
Just listen you.'   But then the old man spoke :
' Horses, and at a gallop ; quick ! drive on !
The road is narrow, we must hold our own.'
And at the word old Larry raised his hands,
And both nags bounded from the whip, then swept

Along the curving road at a hand-gallop.
'Yes, hold your own,' said Greville, standing still. .
The moon was bright enough, and the wind dropped,
But nothing to be seen save the road-turning.
'Our necks are on the race, Larry, I tell you.'
'Tut! never fear us, Master Richard, sir.
Myself saw the bay's dam pass thirteen horses
At Ballydar, and for the mare, belave me
There's not a Prooshian baste can touch her, sir;
Only the twistin of the road might bate us.'
'Confound the twisting of the road! I tell you
If they can catch us—there, by Jove, they are!
Uhlans! Now drive, or we are lost; gallop!'
And Larry galloped, shaving the left rock
To leave some room for lurching to the right,
Where still the smooth road looked down on the
    stream,
A dismal depth below. 'Better be hanged
Than let the poor bastes break their necks that
    way,'
He muttered to himself, true to his trade;
But Greville took revolver, modern-chambered,
From its black case—a beautiful invention,
Contrasting strangely with the great horse-pistols,
Flint-locked, the old man held in either hand.
'They must not take us, Dick,' he said. 'They
    shan't, sir,

The narrow road will bother them a bit;
Besides, I really think we gain on them.
Good Larry, that's the way; good man, I say.'
"Whisht, Master Richard, there's a turn below,
I daren't drive too fast here for my life, sir;
Let us get safely round, and then I'll go.'
Soon came fierce shouting from behind: 'Stop, stop!
Stop, or we fire!' in hoarsest German hurled.
And soon with sharper whiz a ball flew by:
Three horsemen neared them fast at that slow turn.
'Wait till I'm round—wait, Master Richard, wait.'
But one was first; and then the old man rose,
The moon on his white face and long white barrel;
And slow and loud—the sound seemed cannon-like
In Richard's ear—there came the shot, and lo!
The foremost horse fell struggling — staggered—
    rolled—
And with its rider outwards seemed to cling
One moment to the brink, and then was gone
To be crushed both some fifty yards below.
'Now take your turn, Dick; I will load again;'
And Greville marked the old hand scarcely shook.
But Larry held his own once more, shouting
Fierce conjurations at the willing nags,
Who, maddened by the shots and tramp of horses,
Whirled the light carriage downwards like a feather,
Flinging back foam in flakes—holding their own,

More than their own, to Richard's special comfort.
Then self-tormented with the dismal question,
What right he had to slay? might he thus slay
Men who but did their duty—was this his?
Yet much objecting to be quietly hanged—
A precious ending to his German leanings.
But then the road swept outward from the hill,
And there were lights from houses and a fire;
A parting shot or two, harmless enough,
Then plenty of black figures, and the cry
'Who lives? who lives? halt! halt!'

                    It was an outpost
Of Vosgean Franc-tireurs.

               They helped him, tottering,
Now tottering, from the carriage in the light
Of a great torch upon the ancient cloak,
And face so courteous in its withered lines—
The subtler glimmer of its youth was gone—
And many a word and thought was given that night
To the old men of France.

          But Richard woke
Next morn, with free-shooter beside him standing:
Jules Arnaud, advocate and poet, neighbour
Of old, and thinking nearly the same thoughts.
'You here, and not in Paris?' 'Yes here, skewered,

Quite ready for the altar, as you see.
Tremendous nuisance, walking with this thing.
Joking apart, the country wants us all
And politics.' 'The deuce they do ; but why
Out here, and not in Paris ? ' 'She has plenty
Of mouths and arms—of loaves, too, I would hope,
But am not sure.   Here we can eat, my friend.
How is the grandpapa ?   I hear of wonders
Done by you both last night.   Horatius, sir,
On road instead of bridge.   Your Irish servant
Tells the whole thing impressively.' 'Don't quiz ;
You're welcome to your new trade, very welcome ;
Are you yet corporal ? ' 'No, sir, a simple
Soldier Republican.   Come, Richard Greville,
Breakfast in half an hour, and then we'll talk.'

And they did talk, and Richard was talked over
With sore misgivings about Catherine
And that disgusting letter he must write ;
Much doubting, too, that he should look a hero,
And knowing looks are all things until blows.
Still blows must come at last.   And politics,
The noblest cause of all next to the faith,
Called him, he thought.   And so he was enlisted,
And went to Autun for his uniform,
He and the poet, and heard verses read
Something like these :

T

They are coming, they are coming,
   In their columns wide and long;
Marching ever, marching ever,
   Flag on flag, and throng on throng.
And the passing of their armies
   As the scourge of God has been,
As the Hun upon old peoples,
   As the locust o'er the green.

And the scourge of God was on us,
   That we fought to rule, not save;
On the wisdom of our wise ones,
   On the prowess of our brave.
Scarce a back was turned before them,
   We fell ever as we stood;
But the crime of our beginning
   Has been washed out in our blood.

In the blood of our young warriors,
   The noble and the dear,
Soon the time will come, so help us God!
   For wailing and for tear.
Now a sterner task's before us set,
   Free men in a free land,
Where, over the dust of glories past,
   The nation makes its stand.

They are coming, they are coming;
   So to Moscow went before,
Fools who could not read the times, and read
   A destiny was o'er.
Kings and princes, dukes and princes,
   Count and vassal, still half-slave;
They are coming, they are coming;
   They may come to find a grave.

From the summit of our ramparts,
   From the shadows of Notre Dame,

From the squares where soldiers gather,
  From the altar's blessed calm;
By the thousand thousand martyrs
  France has given to God and man,
We have sworn to yield each foe six feet,
  But not another span!

Kings and princes, dukes and princes,
  They are coming—let them come!
Let them drag their great new cannon
  To strike down the spire and dome.
There is rising that within us
  Which will tower o'er them as far
As the peace of God's own country
  Is above man's fraud and jar.

O my brothers, Frenchmen! brothers!
  We whose souls have drank of old
Fire from times when love of duty
  Was as now the love of gold.
Come what will, *we* ne'er shall fail her
  Mother royal still to-day,
Our bright France! nor stand arms-folded
  While they tear her sons away.

And ye nations, foolish nations!
  'Tis for you we strive, for know
The fate of ages yet unborn
  Is quivering on the throw.
Theirs is now the old old story,
  Where the many fight for one,
Stiffening with blood, and greed, and wrong,
  Their own chain when all's done.

Ours the tragedy of stern resolve,
  When millions rise or die;
Ours the faith in God and Man and Right,
  And rightful Liberty.

Yes, ye peoples of the future,
  'Tis for your cause as for ours
That fair Paris stands defiant now,
  Leaning upon the hours.

' The thing was writ in Paris—criticise.'
' My friend, you praised my pictures—*verbum sap.*'

But Richard liked the verses and the man,
Though half dissenting from his German view,
Respecting it in Frenchman—so got measured
And ' tried on,' and the rest of it ; rifle, too,
And wondered would it be like sword he knew of
Some fifty years to come.   Bella had written
Encouragement ; and other letter came
That gave no pleasure, but was treasured deeper.
And he and Arnaud talked of Girondists
With many a laugh, yet honest love the while,
Still thinking it were pleasanter to die
A half-breed death between theirs and the kings
Who paid for others' sin.   And pleasantest,
As was most likely, with their backs to France,
And faces to the foe—there, on those hills—
And mapped the future out most charmingly.
If they survived, whether or not, great future,
A mighty Switzerland of France—strong France,
That chased the Germans to the Rhine and stopped
  there,

Setting a grand example to all men
Of strength in victory—that noblest strength
That conquers all the baser world and self.
Conscription banished from the happy land
That none dare injure, and would injure none,
Where every Ultramontane should be quizzed down.
' An easy task,' the poet said, and smiled;
But Richard did not see the fun, too sore
With those old wounds to take a joke just there.
And then they talked of England and abused her,
And modern wisdom, laughing at past greatness,
A short uneasy laugh—a great fat ram
Among the wolves; ram that had once been lion,
Now calling the old law of common safety
That many just should put down one strong rogue,
' A humbug metaphysical;'—rich England
That still loves peace, but will not dare for peace,
And so will drift to war some day sans friend.

Meanwhile they drilled, and soon the cousins came
To Lyons, taking an apartment there.
And the two soldiers paid them flying visits,
While Richard wondered more and more at Bella,
Gay Bella, who was never gay with Arnaud,
Yet once had been the gayest—paler, too,
And not herself, though scarce avoiding him,
While Arnaud grew worse comrade every hour,

And dreamier.   They went to hospitals,
The girls, and sat up long hours making lint,
And Bella taught the grandpapa to help.
A very fund of laughter and of praise;
But one day, all alone, took from a drawer
A wide old-fashioned album greenly bound,
And in a page that opened of itself
Read verse like this:

> Ah me! Ah me!
>   How cheerily
> The light breeze sweeps on a summer day
> O'er the blossoms so gentle, and soft, and gay,
> That courtesy and flutter and smile on its way,
>   Gladdening each sense
>   With their dear incense,
> The bloom of their joy and the sweets of their store,
> Till you'd think it was summer for evermore.
>   Forget the cold rain,
>   And the shiver and pain,
> And the frost and the snow that must come again,
> Where they in their ruin and shreds had lain
> Till they melted as dust into the plain.
>   So merrily,
>   How merrily
> The soft wind comes and the soft wind goes,
> But it steals the life from the crumpled rose.

' October sixty-nine—the very month
The poor wretch left, and Arnaud he left too.
Could he have writ those lines, planning it all,
Oh man, man, man! could you have done this
    thing ?'

But then there was a step up to the door,
And Catherine entered, shawled and bonnetted.
' What is there, Bell, in that old book of yours?
Something, I know, that makes you cross with poor
Jules Arnaud?' 'Stuff and foolishness; there, read,
Read all the pretty rubbish for yourself,
I've grown too big for it, I think; for lines
I once thought beautiful seem sugary water.
This is not bad, but he, your Mr. Arnaud,
Called it satirical. " *To a fiancée,*"
Whose goldfinch died during the trousseau.
" *Unchequered bliss can ne'er on man attend,*
And fate too oft denies a single friend.
Then weep not, if when dearer love is thine,
Thy goldfinch claims this funeral verse of mine."
Why should it be satirical? You know,
Or ought to know—you being engaged—
Nay, never blush—I wish I was engaged.'
' And so you might be, if you chose, to-morrow.'
' What, to poor Larry? He's a bachelor,
And really rather fond of me, I fancy.
I often did think it not quite the right thing
To have us cantering through your quiet country,
Where the young persons keep as close as rabbits;
It might be scandalous—he's only sixty.
There—there's a kiss for you, and one for Richard—
Though maybe you're too proper quite to give it.

And now come down, for grandpapa may want us.'

But the two men kept to their business closely,
Respecting leaders, yet scarce fraternizing,
So different in thoughts though one in aim.
And soon the dreadful winter froze the land,
And life grew hard enough even to them
With money at their call.   They missed the coup
At Chatillon, and gnashed their teeth thereat;
At many things beside.   Richard lost hope.
' We cannot win, Arnaud; you French are beaten,
Nothing but one great massive love of land
Could lift you now, and that had burst from Metz.
Besides, no telegraph or rail should rest
Within the conquered provinces.   Your friends
The Prussians are too comfortable far
On all the roads they hold.   The game is up.'
' Prophet of ill,' said Arnaud, ' in a week
We shall be back at Dijon.'   And they were.
Aud walked out next day to the ancient house,
And found Annette and blankets in it still.
There had been huge commotion on the night
The horses stole away—much Teuton swearing,
But not much mischief done.   The Lieutenant
And Captain too, despite their savage words,
Respecting the old soldier for the joke.
So Richard wrote they all might come again,

And he and Arnaud shared a room meanwhile.
They sat that night before unwilling fire
Annette had tried to light of green wet wood,
Each cold enough over their cooling punch,
Richard extensive in great coat, and Arnaud
A very handsome picture of a soldier.
The wind outside rushed through the skeleton boughs
And drove in sudden gusts against the windows,
Finding out crevices by weighty volumes
Laid deftly along broken panes—both German—
By Julius, German hater, broom for bars.
A single candle standing in black bottle,
Replacing silver candlesticks with Larry
Was voted nuisance, so the feeble firelight
Threw tall-backed ghostly shadows on the wall,
And thus led on to word of ghost and spirit.

' I quite believe,' said Richard, ' in that rapping,
For things have rapped at me.   I took no heed,
On principle, and so they, tiring, left me
To rap at some one else.   I was'nt offended.'
' But do you really think their ghosts are ghosts ? '
' Not in the least, half humbug, half the devil,
Who wishes to deceive with paltry views
Of mysteries too great for human grasp.'
' We had a joke,' said Arnaud, ' at our school,

That there was ever breeze on All Souls' Day
From prisoners bound for heaven.'

'By Jove, then,
I hope this gale don't tell of awful work ;
There is confounded howl in it I know,'
Grinned Richard Greville. 'Savage blast that last.
Joking apart, 'tis terrible to think
Of all the souls summoned away these months
From this fair land of yours, with rage and hate
Last thrilling through their nerves. I loathe all war,
Therefore I fight, or hope to fight, ere long ;
It is my protest for dear peace.'

'Just war—
A war for country—is a noble thing.'

'The next worst to unjust,' still grumbled Richard ;
'Women and children starved, and souls sent hell-
   ward
Before their time, upon the justest side—
There's nothing fine in war except the brag.'

'And yet you fight.'

'For peace.   Now German gain
Means happy "loot" and wars "in sæcula."
Our cause is cause of brats that are to be.'

'And of the great Republic, Richard Greville?'

'The world's not good enough for it.   Besides,
What's in a name?   Let nations rule themselves,

And rule for greatest good of greatest number,
And call them what you like.   A rose, you know—
But what's the matter?'

                   '*Sacred!* Greville! look!
A face!—there, in that window! devil's face,
If ever there was one.'

               'The deuce!' said Richard,
Making a side-grasp at his rifle—paler too.
'Was it a Prussian, think you?—serious devils.'

'There's not a German for three leagues.   Quick!
  quick!
Which way leads nearest to the door? I'll follow
  her.'

And both the men sprang up, but door was locked,
And Annette had the key; far-off Annette.
Opened at last; a gust drove in their teeth
That nearly froze them, yet they found a track
Outside the study window—woman's track—
And tried to trace it through the broken snow,
But failed; there were so many feet all round.
And so came back under the swinging boughs,
Glad to get in and hear the great door close;
Or Richard was; and Arnaud told his tale.
'The hag that cared me and my country house,
Or ruled us both, until we quarrelled lately,
She cursing me with curse would make you shiver

In that great coat of yours.   She had a niece
Most like herself, but tall, and young, and hand-
   some.
She threw us much together ; having designs,
Or so I think (your sister met us once),
But no harm came of it, at least to me.'

So Arnaud spoke, and Richard felt that night
They were not quite such friends.

                      But the next days
Were busiest days for both.   Germans would turn,
As was their way, and Dijon must be held.
And men began to look to them for brains,
But most to Arnaud, very soldier Arnaud.
Then there was glazier glazing, and next eve
Came grandpapa and Catherine and Bella,
Met at the opened gate with hands and hearts,
And Arnaud fancied that a fair young brow
Grew pink a moment under the bright hair ;
Then strode on swiftly by himself to Dijon
And got his horse, and rode out in the moonlight
Beyond that ancient house under the hills,
Half-thinking to play scout along the lines ;
Much musing too at first on that strange face,
And woman's power of hate in love of rule,
Hate that might plan an ambush in such times ;
Till, as he wound out on the furthest rise,

The moon went slowly down, and he stood still,
Wrapped in his horseman's cloak for the chill air.
And as he watched the lights upon the plain,
Thought verse something like this :

Sleep ! sleep !
May you ne'er vigil keep
    As I to-night.
I, from whose failing heart,
Hopes that were dearest part,
    Like yon faint light;
Yon fading western ray,
Lingering on mountain gray,
    So dimly bright.

Maid, maid,
Greed hath our France betrayed,
Base love of gold and grade.
    Never again
Shall the old triple shine
Wave on the bank of Rhine.
Cursed be the traitor's heart
That from that flag would part
    Now in its pain !

Farewell !
Soon they will come to tell
Of how your lover fell,
    So Heaven befriend.
Though not unmoved I know,
Under its mask of snow,
Quite the true heart below,
    Unloved to end.
He whose lyre, mute ere long,
Hath sung no deathless song,
    Nor made you friend !

Such thoughts he'd thought, riding among the hills,
Whose swelling forms of perfect loveliness
Seemed death-pale bosom of his mother land,
Splashed to his dream with children's blood—poor
  mother.
And ere he slept that night wrote down the words,
And having written, burned them ere he slept.
Why should he write such verse—he, soldier now,
Whose primal duty was to hope; and poet,
To whom truth should be all—they were not true.
The flag of France would wave o'er Strasburg yet,
He felt it through each chord of his French heart.
Greville might talk his wisdom—Greville, stranger --
The land that won such love should make it free.

Meanwhile all things went well at Dijon.   Troops
Mustered in thousands, and the Mobiles drilled
Until it seemed a very place of arms.
Redshirts looked gay on hills—good colour, red—
And most men felt the brave old town would hold
Against more Prussians than were like to come.
So busy everywhere—tremendous Prussians—
Winning at first, still giving to win on.
Yet one triumphant day might change it all;
But day on Loire, at Paris, or in Vosges.
Poor Dijon played but second fiddle, still
What should be played at all should be played well.
So said they as they sat beside the fire

In the old study on those winter nights,
Ere yet the news came of the Prussians seen
Coming one morn to Richard as they slept.
All day the cannon sounded to the north,
Nearer towards night, but with the next day's dawn
The turn changing, backward rolled, though fiercer,
Until one woman's heart could wait no more,
And in her plain black habit and tall hat,
With Larry bandage-laden, Bella rode out
To hear and see and help—it might be, help.
Soon in the deep brown road she passed strange
    groups,
Some straggling backwards, making much of wounds,
But most with carriages of every shape and size
Still facing to the front ; and soon again
The scream of shell made Larry ride up closer
Upon the Prussian side ; then the road turned,
And wheels, up to the hills, and at a touch
Of the white whip the brown mare bounded lightly
Over a rail and cantered down a field,
Snorting a little, and with smooth neck arched.
Two miles in front a very rattle rattled,
And there, through the white smoke, Bella had
    marked
Beside the red the dark freeshooters' lines.
Ere long they passed something from which she
    turned,
All help being over, with a woman's shudder ;

Yet glad no help was needed that should stay her,
Facing for tile-roofed farmstead among vines,
With guess, half dread, that wounds and surgeons
 held it.
A friendly shot had burst the garden wall,
Making an easy gap, but the brown balked,
Its nerves affected by a Prussian shell,
And even as it turned the rider sprang off,
Throwing the reins to Larry. Just inside,
Her head against the wall, writhing in torture,
The stale blood dabbling all her tawdry dress,
Lay a tall girl, writhing without a moan.
With quickest thought, Bella had climbed the wall,
And knelt beside her on the ground. One moment
The wounded woman's great black eyes were fixed
In wonderment, then with red hand she strove
To push the other gently from her side.

' Away ! leave me, Miss Bella ! Leave me, leave !
You know not what you do !

                          Leave me, I say ! '

' But there is none to care your wounds. I'll call
 them.'

' Call them ! call them ! a dog were cared ere I.
What would you have ?—its fair enough, I think.
There, do not gloat upon me—go your way.'

'Gloat on you !. Look, I have a flask and cup ;
A little water trickles from that stone ;
You'll drink, at least, before I go ? '

       She drank,
And with the strength the spirit gave, half sat up
And cursed a terrible wild curse on sin,
And man who sins. For the whole night she'd
 lain —
And now the day was far advanced—in torture :
Struck by chance shell where she had crouched for
 shelter,
Hating the world, and self, and men, and death ;
Half mad with pain.
      Bella had knelt again,
And tried to pass an arm around her form,
Striving to draw the head to her own breast,
Poor black dishevelled head, clotted with blood
Drank from the self-stained ground where it had
 lain,
And as reacting weakness stole o'er her,
Succeeded, and succeeding kissed her brow—
To Larry's horror, standing by the horses—
Kiss that might be galvanic; so the girl
Almost sprang up cursing again. A name
This time—that was not Arnaud's, though well
 known,

       U

And with a lightning-glimmer Bella felt all—
Knew the old crone had lied, and felt it all—
The pride and love mislaid that turned to sin ;
And with her thankful heart yearned to her dying.
' Lean on my shoulder, dear,' she said ; ' the pain
Is very terrible.   Perhaps by and by
We'll get a carriage that will take you home.'

' Home—carriage—home ! I've not an hour to live,
The poor wretch gasped, but holding now a hand
In sudden access of her agony.

' Then pray.   We'll pray together, Madelaine.'

' Pray, pray !   How can I pray, Miss Bella ?   I—

' Who, if not you, whom God hath punished so ?
God who hath died to take away your sin,
And now hath sent that wound in His great love ;
Perhaps hath sent me, too, to speak of Him—
Not well—not as Miss Catherine could, but trying.'

' God ?   Could God, then, feel love for such as me ?
The cry to Him came to my lips all night ;
But I, Miss Bella, how could I let it pass ? '

'Hush, Madelaine! Surely you know the
   picture
Over the side-door in the church—One kneeling
Before His feet—Him risen. She was like thee,
Yet saw Him first—He loved her so. O Madelaine,
Doubt what you like, but never doubt His love.'

'Like me, like me? Lady, the good priest said,
After the first communion yesterday—
I meant not yesterday—who sinned great sin
Slew Him once more in pain. I know pain now.'

'And sin. Therefore are sorry for your sin,
That still hath part in death died once for sin;
And would not sin again if God gave life.
Is it not so?'

         'I would not live—not now.
'Twas kind of you to stay. I like the pain,
It is some little comfort in my shame;
It made you kiss me, lady, and may make
Our good God pardon. It is not too bad—
Too bad—I—I—'

         A sudden tremor passed
Over the poor young form, and it was still.

Bella prayed on, knowing.she held but clay;
Prayed to the God who comes when all have left,
Still thinking of light word she oft had spoken
Of things most His.

                    I have scarce more to tell.
Next night there was a toast by grandpapa
With all the honours: 'Soldier-friends of France.'
And Richard made a speech and Arnaud laughed;
But soon came other news, and laughing ceased.
Still they had done their duty, and that's much;
And by degrees stole down to peaceful ways,
And stood before the altar side by side—
Ere long, I think, the happiest pairs in France.

You might have seen them all one day last week—
And Father Vaughan sharing well-earned breath-
     time—
With the old man beside the lake he loved;
Grouped round his easy chair in pleasant fashion,
Where tall trees threw short shadows on the water,
All shining else with lambent sleepy shine;
One of those summer noons when life is joy
And poetry—the poetry of comfort—
Joy in warm rest, shaded and green and soft.

'Hard day to dream of war,' said Arnaud then
'But war must come again.'

'Peace, peace,' growled Richard,
'Think of your graves at Dijon side by side.'

'While Strasburg calls us, France must rest ignobly,
And France was first of all.'

'Then purify!
Swords red from citizens are weak for foes.
As for the rest, you share the shame with Europe,
Or all her Powers but one. They all helped Prussia
When she was down.'

'But we will raise ourselves;
And you must come from your fog-land to see it.
Victors for hundred years don't fall in one.'

'Nor nation for whom God hath done so much,'
Said Father Vaughan gravely. 'Blood is blood,
Always most terrible, but worst shed inward.
Yet let the past be past, forget your feuds;
Try to convert, 'tis better than to slay;
And all sides strive who can forgive the most
For France!''

' Yes, but the *lie*,' said Bella rogue ;
' There *was* a lie, you——' and she stopped.

' No lie ;
A difficulty—nothing more,' then answered
Richard Greville.

OCCASIONAL VERSES.

TO GARIBALDI.

Leader of the lion brow,
   Perchance of lion heart ;
We, too, would greet you now
   Ere yet you part.
From our dismantled homes,
Where the strange sheep-dog roams,
By dank vale and treeless hill,
And cabin lingering still,
   Greet you apart.

Chieftain in the people's cause,
   Ere by yon ducal door
Again you would enter—pause,
   Or truth is o'er.
Smooth are those English lords,
Courtly their honeyed words,

But not o'er Europe's lands
Are there such iron hands
    Laid on the poor.[1]

Trust not the seeming glow
    That is upon your way ;
Things are not as they show,
    Glistening to-day.
Hard by yon lordly hall,
Where they smile welcome all,
Festering amid the land
Their grim workhouses stand,
    Blackening the way.

Chief, hail thy bark again,
    When their life's prime is o'er,
Such homes have working men
    On England's shore.
Better the aged priest,
He hath a heart at least—
Aye, and a hand to give—
And best, a hope to live
    For evermore.

[1] These words apply rather to the whole system that produces and is upheld by great landowners, than to their individual acts.

Man, know the doom at length
　That's on thy fallen race,
Right must be crushed by strength
　Over earth's space.
He is the people's friend
Who would their sorrows bend
To climb the shadeless height
.Where is undying Right—
　Lift up thy face!

Ireland, 1864.

FENIAN DEATH.[1]

'How BRIGHT the sun is! on those alder sprays,
The liquid sheen shows like a shower of light;
And yonder, through the open, mark afar
The morning gladness lighting all the fields.
Who'd think it was as yesterday the snow
Clung like an old and trodden winding-sheet
To the dead face of earth?   So yet shall rise
The sun of freedom, friend, upon this land;
So yet shall gladden hearts when robber lords
No more may steal man's toil, owning at last
The right of rights is human happiness.'

So spoke the peasant leader; but his friend
Spoke not, and leaning on his rifle, smiled.

[1] These lines refer to the death of Crawley, who fell de-
fending, with three others, a wood in the county Cork against
a detachment of soldiers and constabulary.

'And we shall see it, mocker, from yon sky,
Where heaven leans nearest o'er the fields we love ;
We, too, shall see the fruitful blood we give
Fall like a summer shower on this land.
You've read how once—you are the better scholar—-
A Grecian king stood in the gap to die.
A stag had sold the pass ; but the chief knew
The lives of patriot men buy freedom still,
And so he fell, and conquered for all time.
I would we were three hundred, aye, or—hark !
That's James's whistle from the outer wood.
They come !   Friend, to our posts !—one last shake
  hands.'

A shot, and then another, and again
A sudden volley leaps along the wood.
Angry and loud the speech those foemen have—
Fierce threatenings from without, stern words
  within—
Still sinking riverward these last till now
A single figure steals from tree to tree,
Loading his rifle as he comes.   'Tis he,
The peasant leader.   In the stream he turns,
While many a quick shot sharply circles round,
Stream reddening where he stands.   One last, last
  shot,

In vain, and he is down.   ' Save him, my men '

Yes, weep, weep, Irishwomen !   Braver heart
Ne'er watered with its blood its native soil.
But pray, oh pray, that He to whose pure sight
All human acts are but their will alone,
That God may pardon him who loved your land
' Not wisely, but too well.'

IN MEMORIAM.[1]

'ARISE, leave all and follow Me ; '
   Beside the wave of Galilee
Long ages since that call was heard,
   And hearts grew noble at the word,
Felt their gross earth-stains purged away
   And as the accents broke,
All brightened, mirrored back a ray
   Of the Love Divine that spoke.

And still adown the vale of years
   Each chosen soul that summons hears ,
And rising, girds him for the strife,
   The great undying war of life.
And thou, too, wert a soldier good,
   Thine own words oft of cheer,
And nobly in the battle stood,
   A crown is on thy bier.

[1] The first of these verses has already appeared in ' Through the Night.'

Yes thou to us wert friend indeed,
    A solace at our utmost need,
Are thoughts of thee and of the love
    That still in thy Lord's footsteps strove.
Oh blessed are the clean of heart ;
    They are the lamps of God,
Whose memory lingers when they part
    Upon the paths they trod.

HOPE.

I AM no saint father.   My life—
You know it—grew and ends in strife.
A rough and ready hand always,
Strong, too, and sure.   Whoever says
He struck me fairly, foully lies
Upon the word of man, who dies.
I just had turned to lay my hand
Upon another of his band
In parley like.   For face to face,
He nor the best of all his race—
But there, I grow a babbler.   Now
That hand can scarcely wipe my brow.
Curse it!   'Tis strange to be so weak.
Pray, pray; yes, yes; and mercy seek;
Well, so I do—e'en as I know—
I am no saint; I told you so.

That ribbon on my neck—well, well,
I never was ashamed to tell—

It holds a blessed medal, given
By one long years ago in heaven.
I tell you, father, in the long
Black list of sins if there's a wrong
I have not wrought—and there is one—
I owe it to that gift alone.
The giver's look I used to trace
In the sweet pleading of the face;
It made me soften to them all.
Whene'er the devil comes to call
That same black list, he'll have to say
I wronged no woman in my day.
How my old chums were wont to jeer
About my softness to a tear;
And one—a stout heart and a bold—
A loyal comrade, too, of old,
Lies buried in a gorge up there.
We fought it out, aye, fought it fair,
No skulking side-strokes.   When he fell
I almost wished I'd fallen as well.
But safe and sound I brought the lamb,
And gave her, unharmed, to her dam.
Why, even now, beside my bed,
I thought I saw her face instead
Of yours, father; a kind old face,
That made a comfort in the place.

Speak to me! speak!   Are you still here?
Strange grinning creatures mock and leer,
Jeering me in the mist and pain.
But see, she comes!   She comes again,
That kind old thing, and smiles on me,
And with her comes—Eternity.

LIFE.

A FEW short months—it seems but yesterday----
   And we had parted last.   Life had a smile
For both, but of the two thou wert most gay ;
   The youngest, cheeriest—yet staid the while—
Frank, generous, brave, to all who knew thee, dear ;
And thou art in thy grave, and I am writing here.

The honest heart is still—the bright young eye
   That flashed so true a welcome oft on me ;
Alas ! I'd shudder now to pass it by ;
   The strong form moulders darkly, silently.
Wealth, youth, bright hopes, friends, birth—what
     are ye now ?
The old Assyrian's sneer—the wreath upon death's
     brow.[1]

Such is the life men strive and clamber in,
   As insects creep over a stone that falls ;
Most grieving as they slip ; some laugh who win ;
   But scarce one soul the common doom appalls.
Happy—for listlessness has rust that wears
More than life's cankered joys, more than life's
     cankering cares.

[1] There was an interval of many years between the writing
of this and the next verse.

LIFE.

In life's deep bowl for every joy
    That bubbles o'er it lightly,
There is a dark drop of alloy
    O'er which it gleams so brightly.
In vain, in vain, we'd quaff each bliss,
    And leave the rest behind us;
There's ever close on pleasure's kiss
    A tear that's sure to find us.

Then should we spurn the tempting draught,
    Cast down the cup untasted,
Or, Stoics, feel that pleasure quaffed
    Is time and pleasure wasted?
Ah no! let's love each joy, each tear—
    Aye, to the last dreg, even—
The one will make us happy here,
    The rest is store for heaven.

SHAME.

Fear not to tread !
Men's cruel words have passed her by,
As sweep the red leaves harmlessly
　　Over her head—
　　Fear not to tread !
Hers was the peace in sister's name
Last lingering on those lips of flame,
　　Not hers the shame.

FŒDERIS ARCA.[1]

THERE is laughter and jeer with the chieftains of
    Gath,
  And the Philistine scoffs as he leans on his sword,
For city and plain he hath swept in his wrath,
  And no man will lead down the Host of the Lord.

The Standard of Saul droopeth lone on its post,
  The Captains of David come not to our call,
And rumours are rife of a battle that's lost,
  Of a Faith that was changeless, that's changed
    after all.

Oh God of our Fathers, unchanging art Thou!
  Could the brave ones that died for Thee, die for
    the wrong?
They won us the land, but alas! even now
  Our hope melts away, like the fall of a song.

[1] See Appendix, Note D.

For the enemy flouts us with taunting and jeer,
  And the rust of unreason hath rusted each sword,
Our chiefs are divided in council, we hear,
  And no man will lead down the Host of the Lord.

Hush, doubter! look upward! Lo, where it is
    borne,
  'Mid the glitter of spears, like the sheen on the
    sod
When the hill-sides of Edom rise bright in the
    morn—
  The Ark of the Promise! the Ark of our God!

The ark that o'ershadowed the might of the Lord,
  The ark that the stones of the heathen obey;
The ark that is strong in the power of its Word,
  The ark that our Joshua upholds on to-day.

Now war-horse of Judah be swift as the wind!
  That pledge never failed us and never can fail;
And cursed be the laggart that lingers behind,
  When Israel goes down on the cohorts of Baal.

  April 1870.

AN APPEAL.

Old Dame that sitteth on the sea,
Old Beldame, honest, rough, and free,
    (Cruel a bit
    By start and fit,
And once—but let the past past be!)
There comes a summons o'er the main—
'Tis time to lift the shield again,
And shake that triple spear of thine,
Flashing a glory o'er the brine.

War, war, rides on the northern blast—
But lo, three sisters stand at last
    In equal place
    Of right and race,
Shoulder to shoulder, heart heart-fast; [1]
And though the Uhlan's sword be good,
And Russian stubborn in his mood,
I'll back them turn—well ten to ten—
Before our western island men.

[1] In my opinion a Prussian shot fired in anger would make this line absolutely true—at least it is hard to see why it should not.

Fling out a fair flag to the breeze,
With green and blue in their degrees,
    (Plenty of green,
    For oft I ween
Our Irish blood gave red in seas),
And tell them that from Shetland's Isles
To where thy sunmost coast-line smiles,
From Mangerton to Yorkshire height,
These lands are girding up their might.

With muttered grumble, sternly cold,
The Southern locks his gathering gold;
    Of narrower lot
    The prudent Scot
Counts just once more the sheep in fold;
But fiercer, louder, stronger yet
In waves that bound and surge and fret,
Like mountain-stream from winter's sky,
Bursts Ireland's peasant chivalry.

The quarrel's ours, the quarrel's dear;
France we have loved, and France is here.
    Oh many a time
    In sonorous rhyme
We've almost heard the ringing cheer,
When from those same strained ranks of France
Men saw the old brigade advance,

And stalwart Sarsfield's sword was bare,
And many a squadron went with Clare.

Old times, brave times, still tell them o'er ;
Though none so well shall tell them more,
   Now hard days past
   Grow joys at last,
And they are friends who fought before.
When comrades upon battle plain,
Saxon and Celt will join again ;
For cause was old ere they began—
The cause, oh citizens, of man.[1]

November 22, 1870.

[1] See Appendix, Note E.

PARDON.

ALAS! they're clothèd as thine own,
Those dead along the pavement strown;
In piteous accents anguish-wrung,
Yon bleeding woman gasps thy tongue;
By thee that greybeard's arms were given
To guard his city as his heaven.
Has he, then, broke the contract?   Ask
The soldiers who have done thy task!
Oh Land! they curse thee in their pain—
Thine own—thy bravest—thou hast slain.

Granted they wronged thee—who are sure
To be in deed as aim still pure;
Must every sin be met with death?
A little thing is human breath;
But he who takes that breath away
May quench one beam of endless day.
Mercy is highest trust from Heaven,
But Heavenliest when to brother given.[1]

[1] See Appendix, Note F.

Pardon! Let justice still be done!
Spare not a private crime—not one ;
But they who perilled life and sway
To keep thy sons for thee to-day,
Thus setting pattern unto those
Who should be their more noble foes.
Oh, Mother, give them honour due,
Not death, but garland, laurel too ;
So may thy strengthened cause advance,
So may thy thought be 'God for France!'

June 12, 1871.

ADVANCE !

Awake!
For thy glory's sake ;
For the mighty lines of gold
Where the centuries unfold
Their scroll,
And ever and ever roll
Thy name the first—
There let thy young men slake
Their thirst.
Awake !

Thine, thine,
Sin of the wine
That sent thee reeling out,
Stained wreath thy helm about,
To war
As to new joy afar—
Deeper on him
Whose eye guiding alone
Grew dim—
Atone !

Be free !
All are through thee ;
Shalt thou alone return
As dammed brook from its bourne
      Of all ?
That were the one true fall,
    To lose thy lead,   .
And eat thy heart out, France,
    With greed.
      Advance !

APPENDIX.

NOTE A.

THAT the facts of the case have not been overstated in these lines may perhaps be gathered from the following letter which I sent to the editor of the 'Weekly Register' in the month of August last, but which was not published in that paper :—

SIR,—I will ask you to allow me to reply in your columns to some strictures upon my short pamphlet on Papal Infallibility, which appear in the last number of the 'Dublin Review.' Your contemporary accuses me of having made singular mistakes as to its own teaching. It has never said that Catholics are obliged to obey, under pain of mortal sin, a variety of Pontifical utterances which are not *ex cathedrâ*; still less does it maintain that if we were to get the upper hand in this kingdom, it would be our duty to ' gag the Protestant press, or to annihilate the Anglican bishops; ' and least of all has it asserted that in that case it would be necessary to hang Mr. Husband.

As this last matter has evidently much impressed the writer, being indeed honoured with italics, I will with your kind permission take it first. To my sentence in the pamphlet I appended a note acknowledging that the article which suggested it was not then within my reach. I have since seen it. It dates back as far as

January 1865, and at page 65 I find the following passage :—

'And just as the civil power in these islands would act rightly and laudably in repressing all attempts at the introduction of Polygamistic or Atheistic error, so in those days was it the sacred duty and high privilege of a Catholic monarch to repress all heretical inroads on Catholic peace and unity. So much material force was at all events legitimate as might suffice for the purpose of repression ; and, in estimating the degree of force, one circumstance should never be forgotten, which . on the contrary seems never to be remembered—it is the very idea of punishment that he who undergoes it shall be in a far more painful position than others are. At a time, therefore, that the ordinary condition of humanity was that of severe and continuous suffering, it was an absolute necessity that punishment for every kind of offence should wear an aspect of pitilessness and sternness which very naturally appals the modern " gentlemen of England who live at home at ease." '

I will next quote a passage which is to be found at page 194 of the July number of 1867.

' Sceptical, heretical, and infidel writers, have made the so-called fanaticism of Philip II., in maintaining catholicity as the exclusive religion of Spain, a favourite theme of obloquy ; but his piety and statemanship in using the Inquisition to save his country from the bloody horde of sectaries who were desolating the rest of Europe merit for him the name of a wise, well-intentioned, and good Christian prince.'

Now, Sir, I think these extracts, the precise century excepted, justify me in having written as my recollection of the teaching of this ' Review ' that ' if such men as Mr.

Ffoulkes and Mr. Husband are not necessarily to be
burned in Smithfield, it is because our lives are so much
pleasanter now than life was in the fourteenth century,
that hanging would be bad enough for them.'

.   .   .   .

Since it was plainly right, in the opinion of the
' Review,' to burn a very contumacious heretic in the
sixteenth century, how can the cases of the gentlemen I
have named be excluded from the same rule except upon
the principle stated in the passage complained of ?   The
distinction, the only other one suggested, that heresy
is hereditary in this country, will not, or should not
apply to them, as they became Catholics of their own free
will.   The proposition fairly contained in these passages
I hold to be this.   The punishment of contumacious
heresy in the nineteenth century should vary from that
in the sixteenth inversely as the general happiness of
the two periods.   It is no doubt open to the writer to
assert that I have not worked out the proportion
correctly, and that decapitation, or even strangulation
under chloroform, would be the true finding, but I do
not think that such an inaccuracy is worth being taken ·
notice of, being on the face of it insusceptible of proof.

As to the ' gagging ' of the Protestant press, and the
' annihilation ' of the Anglican bishops, I read in p. 443
of the April number of 1865, that ' If Gregory XVI.
denounced as an insanity the tenet that " liberty of
conscience is to be vindicated for each man," Pius IX,
no less emphatically declares that the liberty of worships
and the press conduces to the corruption of morals and
the propagation of a pestilential indifference;' and all
these ' doctrinal declarations,' we are told in the same
page, possess ' an absolute infallibility.'   Now if all this

does not mean that in the contingency alluded to we should be bound to establish a censorship of the Protestant press, and to pass an Ecclesiastical Titles Bill for the Anglican bishops, the writer should at least tell us precisely what he does mean, which I cannot find that he does.

There remains the most practically important point of all. I wrote in my pamphlet: 'Why even in our own times, and without the same excuse, we have the editor of the 'Dublin Review,' a very able and learned man, gravely maintaining that the Pope is not only infallible when he speaks *ex cathedrâ*, but that we are obliged to obey under pain of mortal sin a variety of his other utterances; and even, I think, the decrees of Pontifical Congregations, which are supposed to have imbibed his spirit.' Now this statement, I would submit, is very much what it purports to be, *substantially* correct. The exact facts I find to be that the 'Review' teaches that a variety of these utterances are *ex cathedrâ*, and therefore to be obeyed under pain of mortal sin, which few others even of its own school have held to have been of that nature, and that one of these utterances commands us to obey the decrees of Pontifical Congregations. All this matter has been set at rest I presume by the Council, which seems to have decided directly against the infallibility of these minor (or looser) doctrinal judgments; a fact which should give great satisfaction to those who believe that the mission of the Church is not to rule the world as the general of the Jesuits rules his order, but simply to guard, teach, and minister to a certain body of truths committed by God to the Apostles.

May I add another word. The editor of the 'Dublin Review' is one of a band of writers whose avowed object is to crush what they are pleased to call 'the Revolution,' by forcing liberal Catholics to choose between their religion and their political principles. The unconscious cruelty of this attempt is almost sublime, but it has been unsuccessful ; and may we not reasonably find in this fact a new proof of that faith which has been so sorely tried in those days.

I am, Sir,

Your obedient servant,

WALTER SWEETMAN.

As an instance of what might at first sight appear to be the hopeless confusion into which Catholics of liberal tendencies are thrown upon this unfortunate matter, I will quote also a portion of a letter of the Reverend Mr. Lavelle, which appeared in the 'Weekly News' of February 25, 1871. The reverend gentleman says :

'As I have reason to believe that a casual passage in my address, extemporised as it was, at the late meeting of the Home Government Association, is liable to grave misapprehension, as being rather vague and too general, I beg to explain myself more fully as follows. Speaking in reference to religious persecution in general, I referred very naturally to the doings of the infamous Star Chamber, some three centuries ago, in these countries ; and then, not to be deemed partial in my censure, I also made reference to the Inquisition. Now this latter reference might be taken as a censure of the Council of the Holy Inquisition, which forms a most important portion of the ecclesiastical organisation in Rome. Nothing was, or could be further from my thoughts than such a reference. It would be both uncatholic and unclerical, and no one would more unequivocally condemn it than myself, if made by another. Not alone was such a reference entirely foreign to my mind, but even any allusion to the Inquisition of former days, as existing outside Spain. I had the Spanish Inquisition alone in view, and that as it existed in those unhappy by-gone days of hated religious persecution. While I love my faith more than my life, I wish, in the spirit of the teaching of our holy Church, to accord to every man that sacred right which I claim for my co-religionists, and of which they were so long denied in this country, entire and perfect religious freedom and equality, a blessing which I hope to see realised to its utmost in my own day in this country.'

' It may be only right that I should add, for the information of the less enlightened, that the Inquisition, even in Spain, was more a civil and political than an ecclesiastical institution ; an engine more in the hands of the monarch than of the Church.'

Now at first sight, as I have said, this letter might appear to attain to the very climax of contradiction ; but I suspect on closer study it will be found to mean simply that the Holy Inquisition was, *of its own nature*, a most important, and quite unobjectionable portion of ecclesiastical organisation ; but that *of its own nature* its power extended no further than the inflicting of that most tremendous of all ecclesiastical punishments, excommunication. In point of fact, the Inquisition, of its own nature, is the very proper means by which the Church avoids incurring that censure for the toleration of heresy referred to in note C.

NOTE B.

That the speaker is justified in this view was, I think, shown by a pastoral of the Archbishop of St. Louis which appeared in the 'Weekly Register' of January 28, 1871, and which described, in an unanswerable manner, the feelings of a large number of good Catholics. His Grace at the same time pointed out most admirably the difference which exists between believing any single dogma of the faith on its own merits, and believing it, as is of the essence of Catholicity, upon the unmistakable authority of the Roman Catholic Church—a difference which seems not to be realised by Protestants, who can not understand how a man who has been opposed to the infallibility of the Pope, can accept that doctrine from the very bottom of his heart as soon as he is commanded to do so by what he *knows to be* the voice of the Church. It may be well to state that Mr. Grevelle's feelings on this particular matter, as I have endeavoured to describe them, were not my own, but I can now conceive nothing more certain than that the Roman Catholic Church has defined the Pope to be infallible under conditions. This seems to me to be so self-evident a fact that I would not know how to prove it. Another fault that may be found with the entire reasoning of these volumes is, that it rests the whole Catholic faith upon the feeling that our Lord was either God or an impostor, an alternative the necessity of which may be denied, and has been very nearly denied in a work of remarkable power which I have only just seen. But can we conceive a man of the goodness and wisdom which the author of 'Ecce Homo' attributes to Christ to act and speak in so misleadng a manner as to

induce the great majority of his followers to become
idolaters almost within one generation—for to worship
a mere man as God is idolatry—and that, too, after they
were assisted by the advent of the Holy Spirit, and
when they were living in a very atmosphere of miracles.
Besides, it is not in St. John's Gospel that we read that
our Lord refused to be in one sense the son of David,
and yet loved to call himself 'the Son of man.'

NOTE C.

It can scarcely be supposed that the writer's meaning
here is that the whole proof of the infallibility of the
Pope rests on this single text. His wish is merely to
suggest that the sudden appreciation of its full force
was the natural means of converting a mind already
convinced that it was necessary either to accept the
doctrine, or to reject revelation altogether. Even without speaking of or dwelling on the well-known passages
to be found in St. Matthew xvi. and St. John xxi. it is in
his opinion to be gathered, from many other texts
of Scripture, both that our Lord wished His Church to
be one, and that He gave a certain primacy to Peter.
Among the faults that are found with the Churches (or
their bishops) in the Apocalypse, is the toleration of
heretics, from which it must surely be inferred that
it was a part of the Divine plan to establish some
authority to decide upon what heresy is. This each
bishop could not be, scarcely even the majority
of bishops, for they might be much divided. Here,
then, the other fact comes in—the primacy of Peter,

a primacy instituted to be the bond of union of the Church—that Church which was to guard the faith. It will be remembered that the proposition contended for through the whole of these volumes is merely that the Roman Catholic position presents, and must ever present, fewer intellectual difficulties than any other position whatsoever. Faith is a supernatural gift of God. One miracle might do more for it than many arguments; but some difficulties must ever remain, or our trust in Christ could not be tried.

NOTE D.

I cannot conclude this volume without raising my protest, such as it is, against the untruthfulness which the modern Ultramontane spirit is endeavouring to introduce into devotions to our Blessed Lady. One fact will convey my meaning better than many pages of explanation. A book has been published, apparently under the highest sanction, upon the co-operation of the Blessed Virgin, in which it is maintained, 'with all confidence,' that at the moment of her answer to the angel Gabriel she had 'a clear and distinct knowledge of each' redeemed soul. Must it not strike everybody that this view, if assented to, would simply destroy the beautiful picture of the Mother of God which has been left to us by St. Luke in those few words which, if they were but the product of human genius, we should call inspired; a picture of which the prevailing character is, if I may say so, its exquisite *naturalness*. Will Ultramontanes never learn that they cannot improve their religion by departing from the inspired voice of the Church ?

NOTE E.

A gentleman was returned for an Irish county a short time ago, who, if his words are not wrongly printed, is in favour, on national grounds, of the practical separation of Ireland from England, while he hopes at the same time that a regenerated France will crush out the national aspirations of Italy. The two views would scarcely seem to be very consistent; but perhaps consistency is difficult in the hurry of an election, and this question of ' home rule ' should be considered on its own merits. Is it so very new a one, after all ? I certainly remember hearing of ' repeal,' for which Ireland returned some fifty members, to the manifest advantage of many of those gentlemen, but I rather think of nobody else; and yet O'Connell was alive in those days. Liberal Ireland has now got much from Mr. Gladstone, and might get much more upon the simple condition of strengthening his hands, by being proud of her rank as one of the partners of this great empire. Why should we not be proud of it ? India was won with blood, very near to many of us. Are we to give up our share in her for nothing ? At all events, England will not let us secede without a war, and she is quite right. If the Bretons claimed ' home-rule' in the sense that some of these gentlemen claim it for us, would they not be very bad Frenchmen ? And yet Brittany is pure-blooded enough to have retained her language, and has neither a Fenian organi-

zation in America nor Orange riots. If it be said that
Ireland had long demanded tenant-right and religious
equality, and that they were granted at last, it can
be answered that they were granted to consolidate
the empire, not to destroy it. Let us strive, each after
his fashion, to abolish the workhouse test for the *deserving*
poor—let us secure to the young farm-labourer a fair
chance of becoming a proprietor, remembering that
property is, after religion, the true conservative force of
the world—let us spread that religion, along with the
blessings of secular knowledge and of art, through our
land—and we shall prove ourselves, as I think, good
citizens, better certainly than those whose patriotic
separatism would seem so particularly ill-timed, except
where it is the result of the loss or peril of their own
monopolies. I speak without a prejudice, and have a
fancy myself that it should be made penal not to have
read 'The Battle of Dorking.'

As for that setting on of France against Italy while
she has a Venetia of her own, it is hard to write of it
with patience. I think it should be remembered that
France rose rapidly to be the first nation in the world,
even in our own time, by leading modern ideas ; while,
from the moment she turned against those ideas in
Mexico, she as rapidly fell. Her natural place is leading
the European democracy. Let her make it Christian !

NOTE F.

It may be asked, how can mercy be 'highest trust
from Heaven,' if to God 'all human acts are but their
will alone ?' and for the answer, as far as I can give one,

I must refer the reader to pages 114 and 115 of my story of 'Onward.' As to the practical effect of such teaching, it is plain that if a man believes he cannot injure his neighbour against the will of God, he must believe too that he cannot procure himself any gratification against that will; while the essential evil of the sin, as injury done to God, remains unchanged.

God is infinitely great, and our minds at present are very small; but I think we can conceive that all things which are in themselves most good are possible to Him, even when to us they would seem to involve a contradiction. Perhaps it is in this, too, that the infinity of that Power consists, whose mysteriousness has been revealed in the Trinity.

In conclusion, it may be well to add that I find that the interpretation of the thirty-first verse of the twenty-second chapter of St. Luke, as given in page 265 of this volume, is made much stronger by a reference to Amos, chap. ix. ver. 9, where the same similitude is used.

LONDON: PRINTED BY
SPOTTISWOODE AND CO., NEW-STREET SQUARE
AND PARLIAMENT STREET